Jacob's Hands

ALDOUS HUXLEY

and

CHRISTOPHER ISHERWOOD

With Introductions by Laura Archera Huxley
and David Bradshaw

BLOOMSBURY

First published in Great Britain in 1998

First published in the United States by St Martin's Press Inc. in 1998

Bloomsbury Publishing Plc, 38 Soho Square, London, W1V 5DF

A CIP catalogue record for this book is available from the British Library

ISBN 0 7475 4050 0

10 9 8 7 6 5 4 3 2 1

Typeset by Palimpsest Book Production Limited,
Polmont, Stirlingshire
Printed in Great Britain by Clays Ltd, St Ives plc

INTRODUCTION

BY DAVID BRADSHAW

The Aldous Huxley who sailed from Southampton to New York in April 1937, accompanied by his wife and son, his friend Gerald Heard (then 'said to be the cleverest man in the world'[1]) and Heard's companion Christopher Wood, bore only a physical resemblance to the author of *Crome Yellow* (1921), *Antic Hay* (1923), *Those Barren Leaves* (1925) and *Point Counter Point* (1928), the sardonic social satires through which he had made his name. Following the publication of *Brave New World* in 1932, a profoundly discontented Huxley had gone to great lengths to recondition both his body and mind, and this process of self-renovation had culminated in his commitment to absolute pacifism in November 1935 and the appearance of *Eyeless in Gaza* in 1936, the novel in which he laid bare his new convictions. By the time they left for the United States, Huxley and Heard were two of the most prominent figures in the Peace Pledge Union, and their main purpose in crossing the Atlantic was to disseminate their spiritual and pacifist creed by means of a lecture tour. However, soon after arriving in America, the forty-two-year-old Huxley was contacted by a Los Angeles rare books dealer named Jacob Zeitlin who claimed that he could 'get him a very good motion picture contract if he would be interested'.[2] Huxley was most certainly 'interested', attracted not only by the fabulous remuneration which such work was known to entail, but also by the possibility of adapting his own novels for the movies.

Zeitlin was given the go-ahead to make inquiries in Hollywood even though Huxley was fully aware that, notwithstanding the money involved, the creative writer's involvement with the movie world was rarely unproblematic and often plain frustrating. He aired his views on this subject in an article for the *Daily Mail* entitled 'Authors Who Cannot Write Films', written a year after he had first visited Southern California in 1926. Huxley had spent a day in Hollywood – 'altogether too antipodean to be lived in'[3] – with the English poet Robert Nichols (who was then working for the movie industry), and it is clear from his newspaper piece that Huxley had formed a most unfavourable impression of his friend's occupation:

There is a widely accepted belief that films would become much better than they are if only reputable writers would take to composing scenarios. Acting on this belief the film companies engage prominent novelists and dramatists at handsome salaries to come to Hollywood and write stories for their pictures. The result is almost invariably the same. The distinguished author is driven to the edge of a nervous breakdown – or over the edge; his scenarios turn out to be useless and the film companies are angry at having wasted their money. Which does not prevent them, a few months later, from beginning the whole process over again with another distinguished author . . . There is no reason whatever why a novelist or a playwright, however talented, should be able to do good work on the films.[4]

Rarely can a 'distinguished author' have anticipated with such accuracy what his own experience of 'composing scenarios' would (on balance) be like. Yet although Huxley was fully aware that his own interests and aptitude as a writer ran directly counter to the requirements of the film studios (who were merely concerned with 'photographically recorded pantomime', as he put it further on in the *Daily Mail* article), it was the allure of Hollywood's 'handsome salaries' which detained him in Southern California in the late 1930s and 1940s. Indeed, he ended up living there until his death in 1963.

Huxley made his second visit to Hollywood in the late summer of 1937. Zeitlin introduced him to his movie-world contacts, they observed a film being made, and Huxley was soon at work on a scenario of his own called 'Success'. In brief, it is the 'fable of how American advertising techniques turn a humble sausage-maker into a national figure', and as David King Dunaway has remarked, 'Huxley was simultaneously brash and naïve in his choice of subject'.[5] Not surprisingly, he was unable to sell his scenario, and by December 1937 the only film work which Huxley had been offered was the task of adapting *The Forsyte Saga* for the screen: 'but even the lure of enormous lucre could not reconcile me to remaining closeted for months with the ghost of the late poor John Galsworthy,' he told his brother.[6]

With the lecture tour completed, the New Year began with the studios continuing to show no interest in the inaptly named

Aldous Huxley and Christopher Isherwood

'Success' and Huxley decided to remain in Hollywood for the time being more in hope than expectation of film work. During a dinner party at Harpo Marx's house, he suggested that he and the Marx brothers make a film with 'Groucho as Karl Marx, Chico as Bakunin, [and] Harpo as Engels'. Harpo thought Huxley was in earnest and warned him that such a film would not be acceptable. '"They don't do films like that here, Aldous"' he advised the Englishman.[7] However, thanks to the intervention of Anita Loos, author of *Gentlemen Prefer Blondes* (1925), prolific screenwriter and 'the doyenne of Hollywood',[8] MGM finally came up with a project which appealed to Huxley. On 22 July 1938 he was able to report to his brother:

> After about 3 months or more of indecision, the film people seem at last to have made up their minds to ask me to do the life of Mme Curie for the screen . . . (It is still of course on the cards that they may change their minds – which seem to have the characteristics of the minds of chimpanzees, agitated and infinitely distractible.) I shall enjoy doing the job – if they leave me in reasonable peace – and it also has the merit of being so enormously overpaid that I hope to be able to save enough in a few weeks to keep me a year without having to bother about anything else.[9]

Huxley was given two months to complete his scenario. He was writing at home (rather than in a studio cubicle, as was the normal practice), and by the time the *News Chronicle* interviewed him over the telephone on 12 August 1938 he had finished about a third of it. He told the newspaper that he had been 'delving into [Madame Curie's] papers' and expressed the hope that it would be 'possible to reproduce the actual methods she used in her experiments' in the film. This aspiration and his sense that his job was 'to put across on the screen a glimpse of how the scientific mind works' indicate just how far Huxley was adrift from the more populist and commercial focus of his paymasters.[10] 'Rather an amusing job,' Huxley told his brother on completing *Madame Curie*:

> . . . tho' I shouldn't like too many of the kind, since this telling a story in purely pictorial terms doesn't allow of any of the experimentation with words in their relation to things, events and ideas, which is *au fond* my business . . . It now remains to be seen whether the studio will preserve anything of what I've done. They have followed their usual procedure and handed my treatment over to several other people to make a screen-play out of it. By the time they are ready to shoot it may have been through twenty pairs of hands. What will be left? One shudders to think.[11]

Huxley received $15,000 from MGM, but he was right to be nervous about the fate of his treatment. *Madame Curie* was not released until 1943, and by then Huxley's 'entire approach to the subject [had been] totally abandoned for what now seems to be "Mr. and Mrs. Miniver Discover Radium"'.[12]

Huxley's eight-week contract with MGM was not extended. Despite this setback, by August 1939 he was again working for the studio, this time on a treatment of *Pride and Prejudice*, and experiencing the same frustrations as before. 'One tries to do one's best for Jane Austen,' he told a correspondent, 'but actually the very fact of transforming the book into a picture must necessarily alter its whole quality in a profound way. In any picture or play, the story is essential and primary. In Jane Austen's books, it is a matter of secondary importance . . . and serves merely as a receptacle for the dilute irony in which the characters are bathed'.[13] This time MGM were better pleased with Huxley's contribution, and *Pride and Prejudice*, starring Greer Garson and Laurence Olivier (and with a credit for Huxley), was released to great acclaim the following year. The success of *Pride and Prejudice* was one of the reasons why, in the summer of 1941, Huxley was offered work on another literary adaptation, this time of *Jane Eyre* for Twentieth Century Fox. As he explained in a letter, it was 'tiresome work, but unavoidable, since books at the moment don't keep wolves very far from doors, and the movie work is on the whole preferable to the continual shallow improvising of articles and stories, which is the practical alternative to it.'[14]

Christopher Isherwood had first been taken to the cinema as an eight year-old in Limerick, and he had gone on to develop a 'voracious' appetite for films as a young man.[15] In the 1930s he worked on the screenplay of *The Little Friend* for the Hollywood-based director Berthold Viertel. Made in London, it was this first experience of working in the film industry which provided Isherwood with the material for *Prater Violet*, his novel of 1945, while Viertel, for his part, considered Isherwood 'a dialogue writer of unusual finesse and tenderness'.[16]

By the time he emigrated to the United States in January 1939, Isherwood (1904–1986) was the author of three novels (*Goodbye to Berlin*, his fourth and most celebrated, was about to appear), the semi-autobiographical *Lions and Shadows* (1938), and the co-author, with W.H. Auden, of three master-works of the inter-war experimental theatre: *The Dog Beneath the Skin* (1935), *The Ascent of F6* (1936) and *On the Frontier* (1938). In May 1939, Isherwood, who had by now embraced pacifism, moved from New York to Southern California with the intention of discussing his new ideological position with Gerald Heard. Isherwood had first got to know Heard in London in the early 1930s, and it was through his fellow countryman that he came into contact with Swami Prabhavananda, 'a Hindu monk from Calcutta who had established a centre for the study of Vedanta philosophy in Hollywood in 1929',[17] who eventually became Isherwood's guru. 'Reduced to its elements,' Isherwood would write in 1946, 'Vedanta philosophy consists of three propositions. First, that man's real nature is divine. Second, that the aim of human life is to realize this divine nature. Third, that all religions are essentially in agreement'.[18]

It was also through Heard that Isherwood was introduced to Huxley in July 1939. At first Isherwood regarded his older compatriot as 'bookish and inclined to be pontifical',[19] but they soon became friends and dedicated Vedantists. 'I think Aldous knows that I like him,' Isherwood wrote in his diary in January 1940. 'This is our only bond. We talk such different languages. Every time I open my mouth he is obscurely pained and distressed. I am such a hopeless ignoramus, such a barbarian'.[20]

Thanks to his connection with Viertel, Isherwood had been writing for the studios since November 1939, and in May 1940 MGM offered him a year's contract. During his time with the studio he worked on at least five films, including the script of *Forever and a Day*, 'a family saga of England made in aid of wartime charities that took seventy-eight actors, twenty-one writers and seven directors three years to make'.[21] Isherwood continued to write for the movies throughout the war years, but from October 1942 his main preoccupation was a new translation of the *Bhagavad-Gita* on which he was working with Swami Prabhavananda. This was completed by the beginning of March 1944, and it was at this point that Isherwood began his collaboration with Huxley on their original story for the movies.

Jacob's Hands was initially 'worked out' on or around 4 March 1944 when Isherwood visited Huxley at his home at Llano (where he had lived since February 1942) in Southern California's Mojave Desert. Looking back on this period in the mid-1970s, Isherwood recalled that Huxley:

> was fascinated by all kinds of rare characters, and there was one, on one of the ranches, a man with the gift of healing animals who was always being asked, 'Why don't you heal human beings?' But he would answer that it might have incalculable effects, and quote the Bible: 'Arise and walk – that's no trick, the trick is really to believe in God.' We wrote a story together about such a healer who did use his power on a human being, with disastrous results.[22]

'It seems quite good and we are going to try and sell it,' Isherwood noted in his diary one week later.[23] 'I hope we shall be able to sell it,' Huxley told Frieda Lawrence in early April, 'as it will solve a lot of economic problems and will make it unnecessary to go into temporary slavery at one of the studios'.[24] Huxley completed his contribution by 21 April 1944, when he told his son, 'Let's hope that when Chris has added his quota, we shall be able to sell the thing and live in cultured ease for a bit'.[25] Isherwood finished his draft on 18 June[26] and shortly afterwards the completed *Jacob's Hands* was sent off to Hollywood.

It was not quite the triumph they had hoped for. 'The studio people thought it quite deplorable,' Isherwood remembered, 'they wanted something suave and cynical. You must understand that mystic doings were highly unfashionable in California at that period. Earlier or much later we could have sold the thing, but not then.'[27] On 28 July a dispirited Huxley advised Isherwood that he had received 'a rather gloomy account of our story' from his literary agent:

> It appears that the reason for the hitherto universal rejection of it is fear of the doctors . . . I have written at length to [my agent] exposing all the reasons why the doctors have no grounds for complaint − the healer's biggest medical success is a moral failure, his biggest moral success is a medical failure, he retires from all but veterinary business because he feels he can't use his gift rightly. Also, the fact of . . . 'wild talents' is admitted by all open-minded people and our story merely accepts this fact and from the premiss builds up a drama where only the moral and psychological consequences of healing are involved, never the medical *modus operandi*. Moreover, the orthodox point of view, that it is all suggestion, is stated by the doctor after Earl's first meeting with Jacob. So everything is safeguarded. As for the crookedness of Dr Waldo − that is considerably less than the real-life crookedness of more than a thousand New York doctors, who are in trouble with the law at this moment for being involved in a hugely profitable racket for swindling insurance companies and the state . . . You might pass on to your agent these simple talking points, with which to allay the studios' fears of the medical Ku Klux Klan'.[28]

Huxley had a point, but Isherwood was inclined to put a more deterministic spin on the studios' response. This was not a propitious time in his life and he had a feeling that nothing he attempted was going to succeed. 'Even if I call someone on the phone,' Isherwood wrote in his diary on 3 August, 'the number is usually busy. I know that, until this condition changes . . . Aldous and I won't sell our story'.[29]

His pessimism was not misplaced. By mid-September it was clear that *Jacob's Hands* had 'come to nothing',[30] and in a later addition to his diary entry for 11 March 1944 (inserted immediately after the comment about his and Huxley's plan 'to try and sell' *Jacob's Hands*), Isherwood wrote, 'We never succeeded. Nobody liked the story – least of all, James Geller, who'd been practically prepared to buy it sight unseen: he was the story editor at Warner's, and one of Aldous's warmest admirers. Either they thought it was too goody-goody, or that it was superstitious, or both. Nevertheless, I still think it really had something'. Twelve years later *Jacob's Hands* was turned into 'a radio performance',[31] and on 9 April 1956 Isherwood recorded a 'tiny windfall from *Jacob's Hands*' in his diary.[32]

The story of this screen story has an interesting annex. While Huxley's and Isherwood's published writings contain a handful of references to *Jacob's Hands*, there is only one oblique mention of another movie project which they worked on at this time. On Friday, 12 May 1944, the two writers had lunch with a film producer named Wolfgang Reinhardt, son of the world famous Austrian theatrical producer Max Reinhardt (1873–1943), 'and discussed *The Miracle*: maybe we shall work on it'.[33] First produced in London in 1911 before an audience of 8,000 at Olympia, *The Miracle* tells the 'gentle story of the nun who falls from grace and the Madonna who takes her place until her penitent return'. It had been 'adapted as a production scenario by Karl Vollmoeller from [Maurice] Maeterlink's *Sister Beatrice* [1910], one of that dramatist's more romantic subjects, idealizing the triumph of the spirit over the flesh,'[34] and it was this meeting with Wolfgang Reinhardt, presumably, that Isherwood had in mind twenty years later when he wrote a memorial tribute to Huxley:

> I went with him once to see a producer who was interested in having us write a film on some religious theme. (It was never written.) This gentleman lectured us on God with authority and monotony for about half an hour. We listened politely. As we were leaving, Aldous murmured to me, 'He's almost *too* spiritual, don't you think?'[35]

In fact, Huxley and Isherwood did 'work on' *The Miracle*, and the result was several pages of 'Suggestions by Aldous Huxley and Christopher Isherwood', dated 29 May 1944 and almost certainly addressed to Wolfgang Reinhardt, which are now held by the University of Southern California:

The Miracle

The fundamental question is, What sort of a picture do you want to make? A historical romance? Or a religious picture?

The existing script provides good material for a historical romance. It has not the slightest religious significance. The supernatural incidents might be replaced by any other unusual occurrence without modifying the nature of the story in any way.

If, as we understand, it is desired to produce an essentially religious picture, a number of fundamental changes in the story line must be made. These changes would all be aimed at making the incidents of the story ethically and spiritually significant, so that the whole may become something more than a mere historical romance – a genuine parable.

The primary concern of religion is with salvation and sanctification; and if we want to make *The Miracle* into a religious picture, we must make all the romantic incidents of the story subserve and be relevant to these fundamental religious preoccupations. A few tentative suggestions for translating these general principles into practice now follow.

First of all, the conflict in the nun's mind between love and her vows must be played up much more dramatically than it is at present. A nun's vows are consummated in a wedding ceremony; she is the bride of Christ. Consequently, the breaking of these vows is an act of adultery toward a divine husband. The decision to break them will cost a woman at least as painful a struggle as the breaking of ordinary vows. There will also be a further element of distress contributed by the conviction (which, as a matter of historical fact, every nun of the seventeenth or any other century would feel) that her act of infidelity would lead to certain damnation. When she decides to go with her lover, it is with the certainty that she has condemned her soul to hell. Her sacrifice for the man is thus of a supernatural order; and in consequence the love capable of producing such a sacrifice must be of an almost frantically obsessive quality. The struggle can be dramatically and visibly portrayed in a series of scenes based upon some of the letters of Heloise – letters in which she says that the image of Abelard presented itself to her imagination when she was praying before the crucifix and attending the ceremonies of the mass. We can have a scene in which, as she prays for help to overcome the temptation, the body of the Christ is transformed into that of the wounded knight. Her passion has the force of a demonic possession, and she is driven to break her vows by a power which she feels to be almost external to herself.

In contrast to this terrible passion, capable of risking certain damnation, we see the essentially frivolous and shallow love-making of the young man. He makes love to her because love-making is his hobby and his business, because (and this is a matter of historical fact) the seduction of a nun was regarded in fashionable circles as the highest form of amorous sport – corresponding to polo or tiger shooting. We can get a great deal of dramatically significant material out of the nun's discovery, when she has left the convent, that the man for whom she has sacrificed her honour and her prospects in eternity is merely a very charming, but fundamentally worthless Don Juan-crossed-with-gigolo.

We now have to consider what happens to the nun when she comes out into the world. As the matter now stands, we have a series of romantic incidents full of action, but without any serious religious significance. If the picture is to have a religious quality, if it is to be a parable of salvation and sanctification, we must substitute a series of incidents that shall have ethical meaning. To do this, we must make each of the incidents show very clearly how the nun acts toward one of the major classical temptations of life – the temptation to which, in the gospel, Christ was subjected in the wilderness. The temptation of sensuality – which in the gospel is represented by the devil's suggestion that Jesus shall turn stones into food – is the first of the great intelligence tests which has been presented to the nun. Subjected to this test, she has failed; in spite of vows and the fear of hell, she runs off with the young man. The happiness she finds as the result of her choice of love is of short duration. The young man, as has been suggested above, turns out to be fundamentally worthless. What the nun has mistaken for deep love turns out to be merely Don-Juanism, and after a number of painful disillusionments, he leaves her – to go off, perhaps, with a rich woman he does not love.

The nun is now reduced to utter despair – to the point, perhaps, of being tempted to suicide. Some almost supernatural incident saves her from destroying herself, and she lives to be exposed to the next great temptation, that of wealth. This might present itself in the person of one of the petty Italian princes of the period, who meets her, falls as violently in love with her as she did with the wounded young man, and finally, to overcome her resistance, offers marriage, which she accepts, in order to escape a life of poverty. In the effort to forget the stultifying horror of a loveless marriage to a half-imbecile degenerate – Italian seventeenth-century history would provide plenty of models for this character – she interests herself more and more in politics, and comes to play a more and more important part in controlling the destinies of a dukedom which, though small, has great international importance, owing to its position as a buffer state between the territories and spheres of influence of France, Austria and Spain.

The death of her husband leaves her in a position of almost absolute power; and we see her at the summit of human ambition, but suffering not merely from her chronic bad conscience and apprehension as to the state of her soul, but also from plain human loneliness and misery. Isolated by her position, surrounded by intriguers and parasites, she has nobody to trust or confide in. She is the victim of her own success.

The final temptation is that of power – dominion over the kingdoms of the earth, in the gospel phrase. This might come in the form of a hinted suggestion from one of her ministers – the suggestion that she should get rid of her late husband's son by a former marriage, for whom, in his minority, she is acting as regent. The boy is a gentle kind of simpleton, with an undeveloped, childish mind. The minister who makes the evil suggestion points out that this boy will never really be fit to govern the state; that for the good of the people he ought to be got out of the way, so that the state may be governed by his capable stepmother, who may aspire, if she becomes sole ruler, to a most advantageous match with some Grand Duke or even minor king. Nothing so coarse as murder is to be attempted. But it is always possible to give destiny a helping hand in the way of arranging accidents. The whole project is made to sound eminently reasonable, humane, politically sound and contributory to the greatest happiness of the greatest number. The duchess does not actually give her consent; but she washes her hands of the whole business in such a way that the zealous minister is left with the impression that she would not be ill pleased if the accident happened.

Circumstances now conspire to make the whole thing go off smoothly and easily. It looks as though the girl would definitely succumb to the greatest and most terrible of the temptations to which she has been exposed. Then something happens – some incident which, though natural, can be interpreted as a divine intervention – something that brings her to her senses. She realizes the full horror of what she is doing – or rather what she is leaving undone and permitting. She knows that the hunting accident, or whatever it may be, is being framed to take place in a few hours, and she immediately hurries off to prevent it if she can. The details need to be invented and worked out; but whatever they are, the significant fact is that she gets to the spot in time and saves the boy from being killed. In the process, it may be, she herself is slightly wounded by the arrow or shot which was intended for the heir.

The net result of all this is something in the nature of a conversion, a sudden reopening of her eyes. She perceives the full horror of what she has done, of what she may be tempted into doing in the future; and she resolves that, at whatever cost to her pride, she will go back to the convent and beg to be readmitted, not as a nun – but as a penitent. This, surely, is very important, if the story is to have religious significance. She must not return to the convent as a last resort, when poverty and disease have made the world intolerable. She must go voluntarily, as an act of free will, when she is at the very height of worldly success. This gives the return real significance. Otherwise it means nothing. She just creeps back because she has nowhere else to go.

It is, then, as an ex-duchess that she comes back – disguised, of course, but still splendidly dressed and bejewelled. And what she takes off, when she resumes the habit of a nun, is not rags, but brocades and diamonds.

Now we come to the final phase of the story. Here again a change must be made, if the picture is to have genuine religious significance. We have to ask ourselves why the

Virgin performed this particular miracle. The answer surely is that she did so because she foresaw that this particular nun had the potentialities of sainthood in her. But in order to become a saint she had to go through the violent and dramatic temptations which her flight into the world provided for her. When the nun returns, she finds herself regarded by her fellow nuns as a saint – she has to live up to the standards of sanctity set by the virgin during her absence. And the significant thing is that she actually does so. The fact that she does so can be indicated very shortly – e.g., by making her go straight from the lady chapel to the infirmary, which is full of plague victims, and heroically tending them. Later, she herself catches the disease and dies – but dies in a state of radiant beatitude and happiness, having finally understood the meaning of her life and the meaning of the miraculous action performed on her behalf.

The incidents here suggested are not offered as definitive story-episodes, but as examples of the sort of experiences which the nun must live through, if her life is to take on the nature of a parable of salvation and sanctification. The telling of this parable will be considerably simplified if we have a narrator. The present construction of the story allows for this. The voice of the elderly nun looking after the American lieutenant can be heard at intervals through the picture. This will have several very great advantages. Long periods of time, which it would take a lot of footage and retrospective dialogue to account for, can be described in a couple of sentences. And hardly less important will be the role of the narrating voice in bringing out the spiritual significance of what is happening and explaining to the audience, what it will not in the main understand, the point and significance of the cloistered and contemplative life. The old nun will have to make it clear to the lieutenant and the audience that monastic life is not mere escapism: that the cloister has exactly the same kind of temptations as has the world – that the Madonna-turned-nun has had to resist the assaults of pride and the will to power just as the nun-turned-duchess has had to do; that monasticism is merely a means for fulfilling the command laid upon everybody to be 'perfect as your Father in Heaven is perfect'; that contemplation is the establishment of a direct relationship between the soul and God and that contemplatives are the spiritual salt that prevents society from decaying, the radio-active particles through whom the divine sends out its radiant energy.[36]

This last, long sentence is particularly notable in that it describes the tenets on which Huxley and Isherwood were trying to conduct their own lives at this time. As Huxley had put it in 1941, 'The world would be even more horrible than it actually is, if it were not for the existence of a small theocentric minority working along quite other lines than the anthropocentric majority'.[37] While Isherwood was completing his co-translation of the *Bhagavad-Gita*, Huxley was preparing his 'anthology with comments . . . devoted to what has been called the Perennial Philosophy – the Highest Common Factor underlying all the great religious and metaphysical systems of the world'[38] which was published in 1945 as *The Perennial Philosophy*, and their 'Suggestions' for *The Miracle* highlight the same problems which must have loomed large as they worked on *Jacob's Hands*. How were they to write 'a parable of salvation and sanctification' focusing on 'the point and significance of the . . . contemplative life', while at the same time concocting a story which would catch the eye of Hollywood's producers and be suitable for mass release? How could they incorporate what was closest to their hearts and meditative minds without appearing to be 'too goody-goody'? Almost unavoidably, there is a disjunction in both projects between the busy, but essentially lightweight, storylines and the more weighty matters on which they rest.

Huxley and Isherwood worked off and on for the movie studios for the remainder of their respective lives, with a great deal of bother and some success, but without ever finding real creative fulfilment. Although he once described screenwriting as 'the most absorbing of all games', Isherwood also commented that 'the films I wrote have nearly all ended in disaster, mitigated or unmitigated',[39] while in Huxley's case the disparity between his own predilections and those of his employers usually proved insuperable. Invited by Walt Disney to provide supplemental material for the cartoon film of *Alice in Wonderland* in October 1945, for instance, Huxley told a friend that he:

> had hoped to be able to bring in something of the old, unreformed Oxford of the eighteen-sixties – but, as usual, it turns out to be impossible to make any of the documentary points which it would be so amusing (at any rate for me) to elaborate . . . It would be nice to be able to reconstruct the university of the period, with its long-drawn struggles between tory High Churchmen and liberal Modernists . . . But, alas, there is no time in an hour of film . . . So I have to be content with bringing out as many of the oddities of Dodgson as possible, and with preventing producer and director from putting in too many anachronisms and impossibilities for the sake of the story.[40]

In the end, Huxley's work was not used by Disney, and the film was not released until 1951. Two years previously, towards the end of 1949, Huxley and Isherwood (together with the screenwriter Lesser Samuels) had worked on their third and last collaborative film venture, *Below the Equator*. It was 'concerned with revolutionary violence in South America', and was largely written by Isherwood while Huxley was away in Europe. But by the late summer of 1950 it was clear that this story, like *Jacob's Hands*, was not going to sell, despite the encouragement John Huston had given Huxley beforehand.[41]

Jacob's Hands is not a cinema classic in embryo, but it is an intriguing piece of work which enhances our picture of the religious mind-set of Huxley and Isherwood in the mid-1940s, while also suggesting, perhaps, the kind of artistic and intellectual compromises both men were prepared to make in order to underwrite their contemplative lifestyles and, more generally, to 'keep wolves . . . from doors' during the war years. It is just possible that their screen story might indeed have 'had something', as Isherwood thought, and if they had been able to work on it with a producer who was both sympathetic to their outlook and fearless of the medical establishment, something might have been made of *Jacob's Hands*.

Notes

1. *The Diaries of Evelyn Waugh*, ed. Michael Davie (London: Weidenfeld and Nicolson, 1976), p. 321.
2. *D.H. Lawrence's Manuscripts: The Correspondence of Frieda Lawrence, Jake Zeitlin and Others*, ed. Michael Squires (Basingstoke and London: Macmillan, 1991), p. 97.
3. *Letters of Aldous Huxley*, ed. Grover Smith (London: Chatto and Windus, 1969), p. 269. Hereafter, *Letters*.
4. 'Authors Who Cannot Write Films,' *Daily Mail*, 30 May 1927, p. 10.
5. David King Dunaway, *Huxley in Hollywood* (London: Bloomsbury, 1989), p. 64. Hereafter, *HH*.
6. *Letters*, p. 428.
7. *HH*, p. 95.
8. *Letters*, p. 272.
9. *Letters*, pp. 435–6.
10. 'Aldous Huxley is Garbo Fan', *News Chronicle*, 13 August 1938, p. 1.
11. *Letters*, p. 437

12. Tom Dardis, *Some Time in the Sun: The Hollywood Years of Fitzgerald, Faulkner, Nathanael West, Aldous Huxley, and James Agee* (London: André Deutsch, 1976), p. 193.
13. *Letters*, p. 447.
14. *Letters*, p. 471.
15. Brian Finney, *Christopher Isherwood: A Critical Biography* (London: Faber and Faber, 1979), p. 44. Hereafter, Finney.
16. Finney, pp. 103–4.
17. Finney, p. 174.
18. 'Introduction', *Vedanta for the Western World*, ed. Christopher Isherwood (Los Angeles, Vedanta Society of Southern California, 1946), p. 1.
19. Quoted in Finney, p. 176.
20. *Christopher Isherwood: Diaries*, vol. i '1939–1960', ed. Katherine Bucknell (London: Methuen, 1996), p. 78. Hereafter, *Diaries*.
21. Finney, p. 178.
22. Gilbert Adair, 'In the Picture: Isherwood in Hollywood', *Sight and Sound*, 46 (Winter 1976/77), p. 25. Hereafter, 'Isherwood in Hollywood'.
23. *Diaries*, p. 336.
24. *Letters*, p. 502.
25. Quoted in *HH*, p. 190.
26. *Diaries*, p. 351.
27. 'Isherwood in Hollywood'.
28. *Letters*, pp. 510–11.
29. *Diaries*, p. 358.
30. *Diaries*, p. 369.
31. *Diaries*, p. 600.
32. *Diaries*, p. 602. See also p. 609.

33. *Diaries*, p. 345.
34. J.L. Styan, *Max Reinhardt* (Cambridge: Cambridge University Press, 1982), pp. 93, 96. See also, pp. 94–5, 97–102, and *Max Reinhardt and his Theatre*, ed. Oliver M. Sayler, trans. Mariele S. Gudernatsch (New York: Bretano's, 1924), pp. 249–322. *The Miracle* was revived by C.B. Cochran at the Lyceum in London in 1932 (with costumes by Oliver Messel and choreography by Leonide Massine) and made into a film in 1959 with Carroll Baker as the Nun.
35. *Aldous Huxley, 1894–1963: A Memorial Volume*, ed. Julian Huxley (London: Chatto and Windus, 1965), p. 159.
36. Warner Brothers Archives, Box 2102, Archives of Performing Arts, University Library, University of Southern California, Los Angeles.

    I am very grateful to Stuart Galbraith IV and his colleagues at the Warner Brothers Archives, and, above all, to the Huxley and Isherwood literary estates for granting me permission to quote these 'Suggestions' (which are published in full). As ever, I would especially like to thank Dorris Halsey of the Reece Halsey Agency, Los Angeles, for her continuing advice and support.
37. *Letters*, p. 470.
38. *Letters*, p. 502.
39. 'Isherwood in Hollywood'.
40. *Letters*, p. 537.
41. 'Isherwood in Hollywood'. See also, *Letters*, pp. 621–22, 627, 630. The present location of this story is unknown.

Aldous Huxley and Christopher Isherwood

David Bradshaw is Hawthornden Fellow and Tutor in English at Worcester College, Oxford and a University Lecturer in English. Editor of *The Hidden Huxley* and *Brave New World* (both 1994), and Oxford World's Classics editions of *The White Peacock* (1997) and *Women in Love* (1998), he has published articles on Bloomsbury, Conrad, T.S. Eliot, Huxley, Woolf and Yeats. He is currently working on editions of Waugh's *Decline and Fall*, Ford Madox Ford's *The Good Soldier*, a study of Virginia Woolf's politics and a biography of Huxley. In addition, he is Victorian and Modern Literature Editor for the *Review of English Studies*.

TO HEAL
OR NOT TO HEAL

BY LAURA ARCHERA HUXLEY

Healing was a subject of enduring common interest for Aldous and me. We discussed a wide range of healing methods: old and new, accepted and not accepted, and even the unacceptable.

Aldous told me that his great friend, the modern mystic Krishnamurti, had the power of healing – but stopped using his gift when people who were physically healed often made no changes in their emotional and spiritual lives.

Years later, in an unexpected and certainly one of the most extraordinary dialogues I ever had, Krishnamurti expressed his startling view about healing. I asked him how he dealt with the problem of alcoholism. He said nonchalantly that it had happened quite often that people, after one or two interviews with him, stopped drinking. When I asked how this came about, he said he did not know. He quickly dismissed the subject and was silent.

His silence lengthened and deepened. Silently, he was holding my eyes with his dark, burning look.

I don't know how long the silence lasted, but I shall never forget its intensity. Then, with overwhelming passion, he exploded:

'Those people who go about helping other people – they are a curse . . . I am not a healer or a psychologist or a therapist or any of those things . . . I am only a religious man.'

Although based on a profoundly different principle, Jacob the Healer also is a religious man. To heal or not to heal is the question tormenting him. To give physical health to anyone in need, to provide indiscriminately the boundless energy of which he is the privileged transmitter . . . should he first heal the body or care for the soul?

For Jacob, this is a true dilemma, for not only is he a devotee of the Pentecostal Church, but also he had the experience of healing two persons whose souls had not benefited from the healing of their bodies. Thus he ponders: should a healer choose the healing of the soul – or of the body? And, anyway, are they separate?

Did Jesus select the recipients of his healing according to the state of their souls? Jesus, who proclaimed, 'Judge not lest ye be judged.' These and other dilemmas float through my mind as I think about *Jacob's Hands*.

This cautionary tale was resuscitated by the intellectual curiosity of Ms Sharon Stone, who read in Christopher Isherwood's diaries of his collaboration with Aldous on a screenplay and searched for it. In a seldom-explored large box full of precious souvenirs, I found the yellowed manuscript of *Jacob's Hands* that Christopher had sent us after the 1961 fire which totally destroyed our house and *everything* in it – only the wood for the fireplace was saved.

In *Jacob's Hands* the authors stimulate questions, present dilemmas, evoke enigmas which I face but am not ready to answer, solve, or unravel. Furthermore, might it be possible that, by now, Aldous and Christopher have found answers and solutions elusive to them when they were alive?

I also wonder if they anticipated the vast changes from the 'laying on of the hands' of the 1940s to the various methods included in today's integral medicine. Back then, healing by touch was generally limited to religious settings, and was performed by what were perceived as fundamental extremists. Now there are two hundred American hospitals where therapeutic touch has been embraced in their routine. Therapeutic touch has emerged as a sophisticated and specific technique with trained practitioners governed by professional associations.

More important, the general area of healing has exploded from the field of the miraculous to the integration of practices from a rich, varied cultural and religious background involving different states of consciousness. It now includes meditation, music, movement, rituals, structured disciplines, and inexplicable spontaneous events.

The dilemma of whether to heal or not to heal is no longer a question. The question now is: to which school, seminar, or workshop I should send my check? Which approach is best suited to me?

Just glancing at my mail, I see the number of choices is impressive: *Healing Journeys, School of Healing, Journey into Healing, Healing Process, The Business of Healing, Stories That Heal, Pleasure Healing, Spontaneous Healing, Psyche-delic Healing, Distant Healing, Healing Sounds, Boundless Healing* . . . and more.

The rich variety of healing methodologies is natural, for the world of healing encompasses everything from surgery to a walk in the country, from a pill to a poem, from scientific discovery to an orgasm, from a well-cooked risotto to a mystical experience, from orthodoxy to freedom from orthodoxy, from a prayer to a gift of money – the world of healing is wondrous and limitless, immanent and transcendent – it is the fusion of Life Energy and Loving Intention.

To many people, the healing experience reveals the unity of body and soul. For centuries, throughout thousands of volumes, the relationship between body and soul has been debated. In just four lines of poetic insight, William Blake, the visionary mystic, states precisely and luminously the oneness of the body/soul in *this* age.

> *Man has no Body distinct from his Soul;*
> *for that call'd Body is a portion of Soul*
> *discover'd by the five senses, the chief*
> *inlets of Soul in this age.*

Jacob's Hands

PROLOGUE

A car is traveling along one of the roads which cross the Mojave Desert, skirting the foothills of the San Gabriel Mountains. Presently, it leaves the highway and turns uphill, along a rough dirt road. The slope is dotted with Joshua trees, striking still, fantastic attitudes. Higher up, there are thickets of juniper.

The road gets worse and worse, deeply furrowed by mountain rains. It winds through a narrowing defile and climbs a flat shelf of land above the canyon. The flat land is cultivated. There are fruit trees, leafless at this season.

The car stops in front of a gate. The driver, a man in his late thirties, leans out of the window and shouts:

'Is this Mr Ericson's place?'

From the other side of the gate, a middle-aged man looks up from the beehive over which he has been bending. He wears the veil and gloves of a beekeeper, so that we cannot see his face. He walks to the gate and opens it in a leisurely manner.

'Jacob'll be feeding the chickens, I guess.' His pleasant, good-humored drawl reveals that he is a Negro.

Bees are crawling all over him. Some of them fly off

his arms, and one flies into the car. Next to the driver sits a woman, well-dressed and still attractive. Her makeup does not conceal the fact that she is no longer young.

She flaps irritably at the bee.

'Get it out! Do something, can't you!' she cries to her companion. Her voice betrays nervous tension, verging on hysteria. After a moment, the bee flies out of the window of its own accord.

'Don't be such a fool, Mary!' the man exclaims angrily. His nerves are evidently as bad as her own.

Crossly, he closes the window and drives on up the road. We see a rickety old house, unpainted and almost a ruin, standing on the rising ground above the trees.

'You might at least not talk to me that way in front of strangers,' says the woman, resentfully. 'Haven't you any consideration? And you made him come to the gate when he was all covered with bees.'

'Oh, cut it out, for Pete's sake!'

We sense the chronic bad feeling between these two people.

The car stops in front of the house. They get out. From the seat, beside her, the woman picks up a round basket in which, covered by a blanket, lies a brown toy Pomeranian, obviously very sick. The woman pulls back the blanket and looks at the little animal. Her strained, angry expression changes to one of tenderness.

'Poor little Topsy!'

She follows the man to the back of the house. Here, in a ramshackle wire pen, surrounded by the chickens to which he is throwing corn, stands a tall, strongly built man in his fifties. His face is tanned, leathery, and deeply lined; with very bright eyes under bushy eyebrows.

'It's Mr Ericson, isn't it?'

'Yes, I'm Ericson,' says the big man. He speaks slowly and deliberately, in a deep quiet voice. His appearance and movements give us an impression of calm independence and strength. The woman feels this at once. She becomes much more amiable, even a little bit coy.

'Well – we certainly had a time finding you! Hidden away up here in the mountains, miles from anywhere! I certainly do hope you can help us – I'm sure we've used up every drop of our gasoline ration – but we just had to come, didn't we, Allan? Oh, this is my husband –'

Jacob Ericson nods to the other man in a friendly, undemonstrative way.

'This is our little dog,' the woman continues. 'The vet said there wasn't a thing he could do for her. Then our friends the Hiltons told us about you. They were here last month. *The* Mr Hilton, you know. The president of the Hilton National Bank.'

Ericson looks blank. Evidently he doesn't know.

'Their cocker spaniel was hit by an automobile. They said you did a miracle.'

'Yeah,' says Ericson drily, 'I remember the dog.'

He comes out of the chicken pen and takes the basket from the woman. He pulls back the blanket and, with

5

a strange gentleness, lays his big, gnarled hand on the tiny dog.

The woman watches him anxiously. 'We should have come sooner. You don't think it's too late?'

Ericson doesn't answer immediately. He is examining the dog, which lies quite passive, regarding him with feverishly bright eyes.

'No,' he says, after a considerable pause. 'No. It isn't too late.'

Husband and wife both watch him with fascinated interest, as he sits down on a bench beside the house. He takes the little dog out of the basket and holds her between his two hands, looking at her closely. Then he lays her on his knees and passes his hands over the small body in a series of slow, rhythmical movements. His eyes become abstracted, and somehow indrawn, and we have the impression that all his senses are concentrated in his big, sensitive hands.

'Just what do you think is wrong with her?' The woman evidently can't keep quiet for long. 'The vet told us some Latin name or other.'

Ericson doesn't answer, but he looks up for a moment and gives her a surprisingly sweet, happy, reassuring smile. There is silence, while he continues to pass his hands over the dog.

'It must be just too wonderful to have the gift of healing,' says the woman, gushingly.

'You think so?' Ericson speaks with a certain grave irony, not looking up.

'Why, yes – I should say I do! Being able to do so much good in the world!'

'Don't you cure anything but animals?' the husband asks.

'Kids, sometimes. When they're little.'

'But not grown people?'

Ericson shakes his head slowly. 'Not anymore.'

'Why not?' the woman insists.

'Why not?' Ericson looks up at them. Then, after a silence, he says abruptly, 'Read your Bible. "Whether it is easier to say to the sick of the palsy, Thy sins be forgiven thee, or to say, Arise and take up thy bed and walk."'

'I don't understand,' says the woman. 'Surely there's never anything wrong in healing people, is there? There couldn't be –'

Ericson doesn't answer. He continues to move his hands over the dog. His face, deeply thoughtful, is seemingly troubled. His lips move. He murmurs to himself, 'Yes – whether it is easier . . .'

PART ONE

The time is around 1920. The place a small ranch, also in the Mojave Desert, but situated on the flat land, a few miles distant from the mountains. There is a two-story frame house shaded by cottonwood trees, together with barns, cowshed, chicken house, and, further away, a one-room cabin for the hired man.

The owner of the ranch is a Professor Carter, a man of about fifty, tall but stooping, narrow-chested, and very thin. Chronic asthma forced him, a few years back, to give up his post in a Middle Western college and settle here in the desert. He is a tense, nervous man; pathologically touchy and cantankerous. Fond of bewailing the decadence of the modern world, of denouncing the younger generation for its lack of idealism and public spirit, he is blind to the fact of his own enormous selfishness. He is one of those invalids who make use of their real or imagined sufferings to get their own way.

Mrs Carter has been dead for some years, and it is the professor's sister, Miss Annie Carter, who keeps house for him. A year or two older than her brother, she is wiry and active; a domineering old maid, with an almost maniacal passion for order and cleanliness

11

– which, for her, is not next to godliness but far above it.

The professor has only one child, a daughter. Sharon Carter is now nineteen, very pretty and vivacious, but so badly crippled by an attack of infantile paralysis during childhood that she can walk only with crutches. She lives with her father and aunt in a state of latent rebelliousness, resenting the fact that they treat her as a rather tiresome child, and longing to escape into a world which her fancy has painted in the most romantic colors.

At thirty, Jacob is a mature, fine-looking man, powerfully muscular. But beneath this formidable physique is a withdrawn and unaggressive spirit; moody, taciturn, shy (especially with women), and thoroughly at home only with animals, for which he has a deep understanding and tenderness. It seems that his experiences during the war, from which he has returned shell-shocked and wounded, have somehow isolated him from the world of men.

He is standing beside a mailbox, at the intersection of two dirt roads, in the midst of the desert. His horse nibbles at a bush nearby. A wooden arrow, on which the words CARTER RANCH are roughly daubed, is attached to the post of the mailbox and points up one of the roads. He takes a bunch of letters from the box and stuffs them into his pocket. Then he remounts his horse and rides back toward the ranch.

It is a good mile from the mailbox to the Carters' ranch. As Jacob approaches it, trotting along the dusty trail, he sees Sharon Carter standing beside the gate. His face lights up with shy pleasure. We can see, at once, that he worships her, but from a respectful distance. She is altogether wonderful; far above him. He scarcely regards her as a human being.

Sharon, maybe, would be less remote if Jacob gave her the opportunity. She is quite aware of his adoration, and likes it. She likes him, too. He is the only presentable male within view. But he is so shy. And she feels almost too completely at home with him. There is no element of excitement in their relationship.

She smiles as he rides up.

'Hello, Jacob. I've been waiting for you.'

'You have?' He flushes with pleasure. 'Anything you want?'

Sharon points up at the almond tree which grows near the gate.

'Do you see, Jacob? The first blossoms. Can you reach them for me?'

Jacob leans over in the saddle and easily bends the big branch of the tree, so that the blossoms are lowered almost to the earth before her. But she doesn't look at them. She smiles rather provokingly.

'My! You're strong! I like to watch you move things around.'

Jacob doesn't know how to take this. He daren't admit to himself that there is any invitation in the way she looks at him. So he decides that she is just making fun of him. He blushes and says nothing. Sharon plucks some of the blossoms and puts them in her hair.

'Any mail for me?' she asks, with affected casualness.

He hands over the contents of his pocket, and she looks through the letters, while he stands by, in mute, doglike adoration.

'Professor Carter, from New York. Professor Carter, from the University of California. Miss Anne Carter. Professor, Professor, Professor. *The American Journal of Hispanic Philology.* How thrilling . . .' Sharon's tone becomes more and more bitter. 'Aunt Annie again, from Chicago. Aunt Annie, from Minneapolis . . . Ah, Miss Sharon Carter!' Her face lights up, then grimaces disgustedly. 'From Sears Roebuck!'

She sighs with a kind of angry self-pity.

'Don't you mind getting no mail?' she asks Jacob.

Jacob shakes his head. His folks don't go in for writing letters. And, anyhow, what's there to write about on a farm in Kansas? Besides, his mother is dead, and the old man has married again and has a whole new family. That's why he came out to California.

'From the prairie to the desert,' Sharon exclaims ironically. 'What a big change! Why didn't you settle in Frisco or Los Angeles while you were about it?'

In his slow, inarticulate way, Jacob explains that he doesn't like cities. He was on furlough in New York during the war. That was bad enough. But not so bad as Paris.

'Paris!' she repeats ecstatically.

And, whereas for him Paris is just a noisy, stinking city where they don't speak English and you can't get hot cakes or maple syrup, for Sharon it is the place where you reach the pinnacle of glory by singing at the Opéra. She herself has a nice voice, and her ambition is to make a career with it – to go out into the world and become a great singer. But who ever heard of a great singer on crutches?

Her bitterness distresses Jacob terribly. There is nothing he can do to help her. He knows she hates the desert and her life with the Carters. She is longing to get away from them – and from him too, probably. She only deigns to talk to him, he tells himself, because there is nobody else. He doesn't criticize her attitude, either. To him it is perfectly natural and right that she should have all the things she desires; and he never questions that she would become famous, if only she could have the opportunity.

'Can't you imagine me,' she continues with savage self-disgust, 'up there on the stage with my lame leg? Everybody in the audience would be laughing.'

'I wouldn't be,' says Jacob, with the utmost sincerity. 'I wouldn't be thinking of your leg at all. I'd be listening to your voice, and looking at your face.'

Sharon is touched. Jacob is really sweet, she thinks.

'If you didn't ever think of your leg,' he continues, suddenly able for a moment to express his deepest feelings, 'nobody else would either. There's that dog over at the Blue Star Ranch that got hurt last fall. He doesn't sit in a corner and say, "I'm a cripple." He runs around with the others, the best way he can –'

He stops abruptly, realizing that he has implied a criticism of Sharon's attitude to life. But Sharon isn't displeased. There are occasions, like this, when she feels that Jacob isn't just another hick, a cowhand, a dumb farm boy. He has his own human dignity, his philosophy of experience. Perhaps he is something more than any of them imagine. Then she shakes her head sadly.

'You wouldn't laugh, Jacob. I know that. You're different. You're not like the people in the cities. They're so – sophisticated.'

'I haven't had much of an education,' Jacob agrees slowly. 'But I can't see that folks are clever just because they find fault with everything.'

Sharon sighs, and says she must go and take the mail to her father. Jacob mounts his horse again and, when she asks him where he's going, explains that he has to look for two of the calves which have gone off with Pearce's cattle. If he doesn't bring them back now, they'll be wandering all over the desert. He rides off. Sharon watches him out of sight, smiling to herself. Her talk with Jacob, as always, has somehow raised her spirits. She hardly knows why. He is like that. There is something comforting about him.

She turns and walks on her crutches back to the house. Crossing the porch, she enters the living room, where she finds her father, sitting at the table, reading a thick book and making notes on cards, which he puts from time to time into a file. He wears an overcoat, although there is a large stove in the room.

He looks up sharply as the door opens and pulls his coat closer across his chest.

'Shut that door!' he calls, testily.

She does so; then lays the letters on the table.

'Here's your mail, Father,' she says. Then, making a special effort to be nice to him, she holds out the sprig of almond blossoms.

'Isn't that lovely! The first this year.'

But instead of inhaling the fragrance, her father knocks the flowers out of her hand. Does she want to bring on an attack of his asthma with that filthy pollen? And there's the draft – why can't she shut the door? He pulls up his coat collar and goes into a fit of coughing.

Her happy enthusiasm quite extinguished, Sharon limps back to the door and closes it.

'I'm sorry,' she says, but her tone is resentful.

Professor Carter makes a few remarks about the thoughtless selfishness of young people, then goes back to his reading.

Sharon takes off her things and goes over to the piano.

'Would it disturb you if I practiced my singing?' she asks.

'No, no. Go ahead,' says the professor, with the expression of a martyr. As she starts to play and sing, he takes a wad of cotton from his pocket and stuffs a piece in either ear.

17

Voices are heard in the kitchen, and Miss Carter pops her head in and calls to her brother. He doesn't hear her the first time, and she has to call again. He looks up, removes the cotton, and asks her what she wants.

'It's Tom Pearce,' she says, 'from the Tillman Ranch.'

Professor Carter goes out into the kitchen. Tom Pearce, foreman of the big cattle ranch nearby, explains his business. He has come over to look at the sick calf in the professor's barn. Hind legs paralyzed, high fever, collapse – there can't be any doubt. It is a case of what cattlemen call black quarter. And what worries Pearce is that two of his own calves have begun to show suspicious symptoms.

Sharon, who has come into the kitchen to listen, asks if the disease is fatal, and is told that the calf will certainly be dead within two days. 'Poor Jacob!' she exclaims. For, to him, the calf was almost a pet. He would be brokenhearted if anything happened to it.

This remark gets her another lecture from the professor, who reminds her that this kind of sentimentality is often a form of cruelty. The animal must be put out of its misery at once. Looking out of the window, he sees Jacob riding home with the cattle. He tells Sharon to go and order him to kill the calf right away.

Sharon goes out and calls to Jacob, who dismounts and comes to meet her. She tells him what Pearce has said and passes on her father's orders. Jacob looks so utterly miserable that she instinctively lays a comforting hand upon his arm, but he hardly seems to notice her.

'I'm so terribly sorry, Jacob,' she tells him. 'I wish there was something we could do.'

Jacob turns from her abruptly. There are tears in his eyes. She goes back into the house.

Jacob ties his horse and lets himself into the stall where the sick calf is lying in the straw. He kneels down beside it and in a low voice begins to talk to it.

'You're not going to die,' he keeps repeating. 'I won't let you die. I won't let you.'

The intensity of his emotion makes him tremble; the hands with which he strokes the sick animal are shaking. Then he clenches his fists, makes a great effort to control himself. Having regained his calm, he lays his hands once again on the calf. 'I won't let you die,' he goes on muttering, again and again, as he passes his hands over the calf's body.

Suddenly the creature stirs a little and, a moment later, struggles to its feet.

Kneeling on the straw, Jacob stares at it with wide astonished eyes.

The calf starts to low. Jacob gets up, goes out of the stall, pours some milk from a pail into a tin pan, and then comes back. He dips his finger in the milk, gives it to the calf to suckle. He repeats this two or three times and finally gets the little animal to drink direct from the pan.

While this is happening, voices are heard outside. The door of the stall is opened, and Tom Pearce and Sharon appear on the threshold.

Flabbergasted by what he sees, Pearce questions Jacob. What happened? How did he do it? Jacob can give no rational answer. He was just stroking the calf, and it got up and started hollering for milk.

Next day, Pearce brings his own sick calves over to the Carter Ranch in a truck. With him rides a small boy, holding a mongrel puppy with one of its legs in a splint. News of the cure has spread around, and there is an audience of curious neighbors to watch Jacob as he successfully treats all the animals. The small boy is in raptures of delight. Pearce offers Jacob some money as a fee for his services, but Jacob refuses it. 'It's not anything *I* do,' he keeps repeating. 'It just comes into me, somehow. It's as if I can feel it, going out through my hands.'

The attitude of Professor Carter and his sister is suspicious and disapproving. Miss Annie thinks it very peculiar – perhaps not even Christian. The professor is convinced that it must either be a fraud, or else the worst kind of unscientific superstition. He takes Pearce aside and asks his advice. Does he think it safe for him to keep a man like Jacob in his employ? Oughtn't the fellow to be fired immediately?

Pearce reassures him. Jacob, he says, is an honest boy – and, scientific or superstitious, the fact remains that some people do have this gift of healing. He himself has known an old Indian who could cure rheumatism.

Throughout all this excitement and discussion, Sharon keeps in the background, listening and watching. Her face is tense and pale with excitement – as if she were a bit scared by her own thoughts.

That evening, Jacob is sitting alone in his cabin, mending a saddle by the light of a kerosene lamp. As he works, a tame squirrel, another of his pets, runs over him, dives into the pocket of his jacket and emerges with a peanut which it starts to eat, perched on his shoulder.

There is a rap on the windowpane. He looks up and sees Sharon. He opens the door, obviously embarrassed by this late visit, and certain that it could only be caused by some emergency.

'Is anything wrong at the house?' he asks.

'No. Nothing. Let me in. I've got to talk to you.'

She is in a state of great emotional tension – having, in fact, come to a dramatic decision. She takes little notice of Jacob's solicitous fussing. He dusts off the chair with his sleeve and apologizes several times for the untidiness of the cabin. She limps into the middle of the room and sits down. There is an expectant pause. Then she turns to Jacob and speaks rapidly in a trembling voice, as if delivering an ultimatum:

'Jacob, you've got to help me. I watched you. I know you can do it. You've got to cure me!'

He gapes at her. 'Cure you?'

'Like you did those animals.'

'But – but that was different.'

'Why is it different?' Sharon asks, almost fiercely.

Incoherently, Jacob tries to explain. Animals are

21

animals. You just feel sorry for them because they're so helpless. And you feel how dependent they are on you – how they care for you, and you care for them . . .

'Don't you care for *me*, Jacob?'

He averts his eyes in an agony of shyness. But Sharon, in the extremity of her need, has no time for coquetry and pretenses.

'Don't you care for me – more than anybody or anything?'

He looks up and turns his head away.

'You know I do!' he blurts out.

'Then you'll help me!' she exclaims, triumphantly.

He still hesitates. He mutters that he doesn't know how.

'Kneel down,' she tells him imperiously, pointing to the floor beside her chair.

Sheepishly, he does as he is told.

'Now do it. Do what you did to the calf.'

Still he hesitates.

'Take my foot. Take it in your hands.'

But he can't. Something holds him back. He is trembling all over.

'What's the matter?' she exclaims in bitter desperation. 'Don't you want to touch it? Because it's so ugly?'

Jacob gives a kind of moan of pain and tenderness. He bends down and touches the poor, twisted ankle with his lips.

'Jacob,' she says pleadingly, 'make it well. I know you

can if you really want to. I have faith even if you haven't. It *must* be possible . . . I want to be able to walk. I want to run and dance. I want to be like other people. Do it for me, Jacob . . .'

Slowly, he raises his big hands. They remain poised for a moment above her foot; then, very gently, they close around it.

Sharon closes her eyes. She seems to be trying to relax, to give herself up, completely, to his will and thus cooperate with the effort he is making.

Jacob begins to pass his hands over the twisted limb.

'Don't let her limp anymore,' he murmurs. 'She's going to get well. She's going to get strong and well . . .'

And Sharon herself with closed eyes also murmurs, 'I'm going to get well, I know it. I'm going to get well . . .'

Then they are both silent, and Jacob's hands continue to move.

At last, he stops. He seems exhausted, as if by a tremendous emotional crisis.

'Try it now,' he tells her, almost in a whisper.

Slowly, cautiously, Sharon raises herself from the chair and tries to stand. Her face lights up as if she feels a new strength in the withered limb. An exclamation of delight breaks from her lips. She takes a step forward.

Then the crippled foot gives way under her, and she has to catch hold of Jacob's arm to prevent herself from falling. Her face contorts. She winces with pain.

They look at each other. Jacob averts his eyes.

'I'm sorry . . .' he mutters.

Sharon takes up her crutches.

'It's late,' she says in a toneless voice. 'I guess I'd better be going . . .'

'Sharon . . .'

'You did your best. Thank you . . .' She lays her hand on his arm, tries pathetically to smile, but her lips are trembling. 'I'm such a fool. I hoped . . .' She turns from him quickly. She is crying.

'Sharon . . .' He is terribly distressed. 'I tried . . .'

He wants to help her, but she pushes him aside, sobbing. Crushed by her enormous disappointment, she limps out of the cabin and disappears into the darkness.

Very early next morning, Jacob is up milking.

We see from his face that he is still shaken by the experiences of the previous night. He murmurs to himself. The cow turns her head toward him, and – as always when he is with animals – we get the impression that a curious understanding and sympathy exist between them.

Suddenly we hear Sharon's voice, wild with excitement.

'Jacob!' she calls. 'Jacob!'

He looks up, jumps to his feet.

Then we see Sharon herself. Joy makes her face radiant, scarcely recognizable. She is running toward him, breathless, without her crutches or a trace of her limp. With a bound, she crosses the irrigation ditch.

24

'Jacob! Jacob! Look at me!'

The next moment she has thrown herself into his arms and is kissing him.

Jacob stands there, paralyzed with amazement. Then slowly he understands what has happened. His arms go around her. He kisses her, not so much with passion as in a rapture of delight and gratitude.

'Sharon! Are you out of your mind?'

It is Miss Annie, who has come out of the house in time to witness this tableau with horrified astonishment. But before she can open a tirade of denunciation, Sharon effectively distracts her thoughts by breaking from Jacob's embrace and running toward her.

'Aunt Annie! Look! I'm cured!'

And she rapturously kisses her aunt.

The picture is completed by Professor Carter, who puts his head angrily out of the bedroom window, to know what all the noise is about so early. He takes in the scene. Sharon demonstrates her recovery by dancing a wild jig and blowing him kisses.

The news of Sharon's healing spreads fast over the desert grapevine. Two days later the Carters are visited by a doctor from the nearest town who is curious to investigate this miracle for himself. Professor Carter doesn't welcome the intrusion, but there is nothing he can do to prevent it, except to treat the whole affair as lightly as possible. He suggests that Sharon's paralysis has never been severe, that the limb was not in the least deformed, that the disability was probably hysterical in origin, and so forth. Nevertheless, we can see that his scientific certainties have been badly shaken; and that something frightens him – the element of the unknown power which seems to reside in Jacob. He refers quite resentfully to his hired man.

The doctor, of course, wants to see Jacob. He is sent for, and there is a most unsatisfactory cross-examination. Jacob is at his most inarticulate. Medical words are fired at him, and he reacts blankly. Does he employ hypnosis? Does he know what hypnosis is?

Jacob doesn't know anything. He can't explain. He isn't even sure that he is responsible for Sharon's cure. When he tried that night, it didn't work. This, of course, brings to light the fact that Sharon has visited Jacob's cabin – a detail which seems more significant to Miss Annie than the cure itself. She questions Jacob sharply, revealing her worst suspicions. Jacob is first puzzled and then shocked at the suggestion. Miss Annie feels that she is on the right track. She tells the doctor that she and her brother have already decided to send Sharon away for a while, to a cousin, a minister in the Middle West. She needs a strict eye upon her and wholesome Christian influences.

But the doctor is no fool. He is really interested. And now he asks to see Sharon herself. He would like to make an examination of the limb. Professor Carter is unwilling, but the mention of Sharon reminds Miss Annie that they haven't seen her all day. She must be out, roaming around the desert. This new freedom is disagreeable to both father and aunt; and is, in itself, a good reason why the girl should be placed under greater restraint. Miss Annie is so busy that she will never be able to keep an eye on her, now that she isn't handicapped by her crutches.

Jacob, however, is seriously alarmed. Sharon may have overtaxed her strength. The power to move about freely is so new to her. Perhaps she has fallen somewhere, or fainted. And the desert is swarming with rattlesnakes. He offers to ride out and look for her. The Carters are unwilling, but there is nobody else to send, so they agree.

When Jacob has left the room, they tell the doctor that they have decided to fire him as soon as they can get another man. He is queer and undesirable and not to be trusted with girls.

Jacob, meanwhile, returns to his cabin to get his saddle.

He opens the door. There is a note pinned on the inside in Sharon's handwriting.

Dear Jacob,

I am going away. I wanted to see you before I left, but you weren't around, and I had to hurry. I'm going to Los Angeles, to get a job and try to be a singer and do all those things we used to talk about. It's no use Father and Aunt Annie coming after me. Even if they find me, I won't come back. I know where they're planning to send me. If I don't go now, I won't get another chance.

I owe everything to you, Jacob. And I'll never forget that. One day I'll pay it all back to you, and more. But first I'm going to make good. I know you want me to. Wish me luck.

Love,
Sharon

PART TWO

PART TWO

About eighteen months later.

It is evening. Carrying a sick child in his arms, a colored man, whom we shall later identify as George, the Medwins' chauffeur, turns out of Main Street in downtown Los Angeles into a dark alley. Beside him walks a colored woman, his sister, the mother of the sick child. A few yards from the corner of Main Street, they come to a shabby wooden building, on which is painted the name: CHURCH OF THE PRIMITIVE PENTECOSTAL BROTHERHOOD. They enter.

The church is a small bare hall with a raised platform at one end and rows of benches for the congregation. The place is crowded. There are Negroes, Mexicans, Chinese, and a sprinkling of Caucasians; all poor, simple, devout people.

The minister, Reverend Wood, an old Negro with gray hair, is just at the end of his sermon. His earnest eloquence is at once touching in its sincerity; absurd because of his queer locutions and quaintly applied texts. The congregation expresses its feelings with periodical cries of 'Hallelujah! Amen! Glory!'

The sermon comes to an end, and the minister

announces that Brother Ericson is again in their midst and will demonstrate healing as on previous Thursday evenings. Jacob, who has been sitting in a dark corner behind the pulpit, comes shyly forward. He is dressed in working overalls, for he has come straight from his job and has had no time to change.

There is a scramble toward the platform, mostly of parents with sick or crippled children. Jacob and the minister try to bring order to the unruly throng pressing about them. One at a time, please. No pushing. Remember that this is God's house, not the circus.

In stammering, incoherent phrases, Jacob explains that he can't guarantee a cure. Sometimes it happens, sometimes it doesn't. And when it does happen, the cure doesn't always take place immediately. Sometimes it may be delayed for hours, or days, or even weeks.

The minister helps him out in these explanations, giving a theological turn to his simple statements of fact. The Lord works in mysterious ways. Many are called but few are chosen. And so forth. Finally, Reverend Wood calls for a hymn. The harmonium starts to wheeze, and while the congregation sings ecstatically, the work of healing begins.

First, an old blind woman is touched without any apparent result. Then it is the turn of the child whom we saw carried into the church by George, the colored chauffeur, at the beginning of this sequence. It is a case, the mother explains, of abscesses of the ears. The child is moaning with pain. Jacob passes his hands over her several times. Suddenly, she stops crying and begins to laugh. The congregation is delighted. There is much excitement and an outburst of hallelujahs.

Meanwhile, these proceedings are being closely watched by a man who sits alone in the back row. It is obvious at a glance that he is not a regular member of the congregation. Mr Lou Zacconi is a plump, flashily dressed individual of forty; handsome in a vulgar way, with fat white hands, on which he wears several large rings. He has a curly black moustache and dark, bright, dishonest eyes.

During the sermon, Zacconi has been undisguisedly bored and restless. At one moment, he even pulls a large cigar out of his breast pocket and is about to light it, when he remembers that he is in a church and sticks it back again with a muttered curse of annoyance.

But when the healing begins, he leans forward to watch with eager interest. As soon as the service is over, he pushes his way through the outgoing crowd and waylays Jacob, who is being steered out of the building by the old minister.

'Mr Jacob Ericson, I believe?' Zacconi takes no notice whatever of Reverend Wood. 'It's a pleasure to meet you, sir. I'm Lou Zacconi. You don't know me, but I'm quite a fan of yours. Yes, sir!'

Jacob obediently takes the card which Zacconi offers him and examines it. We read that Mr Zacconi is the 'Sole Lessee and Manager of the Main Street Art Theater.'

'It's a great job you're doing, Mr Ericson,' Zacconi continues. 'A wonderful job. The public ought to know about it. I'd appreciate it very much if I could have a talk with you. Can you spare me a few minutes? I have several angles I think might interest you.'

Reverend Wood, who evidently knows plenty about Mr Zacconi already, and nothing to his credit, tells him mildly that Jacob is always tired after the healing and needs a rest. But Zacconi cuts him short.

'Sure. Sure, I know that. Just you step over to my office, Mr Ericson. You can relax all you want to.'

And, without more ado, he takes the bewildered young man's arm and leads him off.

On the way to the office, Zacconi talks fast, unfolding his schemes. Jacob is wasting his time in that outfit. He needs backing, he needs a manager, he needs a wider audience.

'Look at it this way. You've got something to give to the public. Well, I've got the public that wants to have it. You do your job. You don't want to be bothered with a lot of business details. Of course you don't. I appreciate that. I respect your attitude. But just the same you have to put things on a sound business basis . . .'

Jacob scarcely knows what Zacconi is talking about. Occasionally, he tries to ask a question, but he doesn't succeed in checking the showman's fluent phrases.

Meanwhile, they turn into Main Street and find themselves in front of the Art Theater, a gaudy little place, whose front seems to be built entirely of billboards and electric lights, displaying the names and curves of the showgirls who take part in a nonstop performance of cheap vaudeville and burlesque. Mr Zacconi's public is almost exclusively male, and is recruited largely from sailors, high school kids, and out-of-town visitors who have come to gape at the fleshy delights of the big city.

Smoking, perspiring, and breathing heavily, most of them in their shirtsleeves, they follow the performance with greedy eyes. Instead of the hallelujahs of the Reverend Wood's congregation, there are catcalls, whistles, explosions of hoarse laughter, and bursts of clapping.

Zacconi leads the way down a side aisle to a door which gives access to the backstage regions of the theater. On the stage, two enormous females in spangled tights are doing a wrestling act, which includes deliberate and indecent accidents to intimate parts of their costumes, and thunderous pratfalls. The audience yells encouragement.

Jacob, who has been following Zacconi, halts and gapes at the scene in naïve bewilderment. Then he, too, begins laughing heartily. Zacconi turns impatiently and fairly pushes him through the backstage door. Elbowing their way past sceneshifters and weary chorus girls, they reach the manager's office and enter.

'Hello, Doc,' says Zacconi, to the man who rises to greet them, and he presents Jacob to his old and valued friend, Dr Ignatius Waldo.

Dr Waldo is a small man in his fifties, with a sharp ferret-face and darting little eyes behind a pair of pince-nez at the end of a broad black ribbon. He wears seedy black clothes, a stick-up collar and bow tie. But in spite of his efforts to dress and act the part of a successful professional man, he looks what in fact he is – an unsuccessful and extremely shady physician, in bad odor with the Medical Association and only just on the right side of the law.

Dr Waldo is much more pompous and sententious than Zacconi. He speaks gravely, in a deep voice which doesn't fit his physique. He tells Jacob that he has heard all about him and his wonderful powers from Mr Zacconi. He is greatly interested. As an open-minded scientist, he has always felt that doctors should cooperate with genuine healers. A wonderful partnership could be built up by a genuine healer working with an ethical man of medical science. ('Ethical' and 'scientific' are Dr Waldo's favorite words. They keep recurring as a sort of leitmotiv in his conversation, which is enriched by all the medical and philosophical terms he knows, including many he can't pronounce.)

Pretty soon they get down to business – for it is evident that the two men have worked out their proposition in advance. The three are to go into partnership. Jacob is to contribute the healing; Doc the ethics and science (in other words, the necessary front of medical respectability); and Zacconi the capital and the management. Profits are to be divided on the basis of fifty percent for Zacconi, thirty for Doc, and twenty for Jacob, who will be given free board and lodging. This last is stressed very strongly, as though it were a bit of unparalleled generosity. Doc and Jacob will set up their joint office in a suitable location. Three times a week, Jacob is to give demonstrations of his talent at the Main Street Art Theater.

Jacob doesn't like the idea at all. He has a job already, and is making enough to satisfy his simple needs. He doesn't want to leave Reverend Wood. And he absolutely refuses to do his healing on the stage. 'It wouldn't be right,' he keeps repeating.

'But you did it in that church,' says Zacconi.

'That's different,' Jacob insists. 'It wasn't for money.'

'What's wrong with my show anyway? It's a nice, artistic show. Nothing vulgar about it. If you like, we'd have the orchestra play something religious. "Ave Maria."'

'I'm sorry, Mr Zacconi,' says Jacob, somewhat distressed. 'You're being very generous, I know. But I couldn't do it. It just wouldn't be right.'

And, despite all their arguments and persuasions and growing exasperation, he sticks to his guns.

In the midst of this discussion, at a point when it seems that complete deadlock has been reached, there is a knock on the door.

'Come in,' Zacconi calls irritably. Then, when he sees who it is: 'Sorry, kid. Can't see you now. I'm busy.'

But Jacob has jumped to his feet. 'Sharon!' he exclaims.

And, indeed, it is Sharon herself, though at first glance we scarcely recognize her. She has changed very much from the girl on the Carter Ranch. She looks much older and more mature, in the low-necked, long-skirted evening gown which marks her off from the half-naked chorus girls as a featured blues singer. She looks tired, too, and her manner is harder. She has been learning things, not always in the easiest way. But her face lights up when she sees Jacob. She is nearly as pleased as he is. Nearly, but not quite. It is plain that she is dismayed to find him in this atmosphere.

'Why, Jacob, what in the world are you doing here?'

'You know Miss Dolores?' Zacconi asks in surprise.

'Dolores?' Jacob is puzzled. Then he inquires anxiously, 'Did you get married or something?'

Sharon laughs, somewhat bitterly. 'Only to my art. Zacconi thought Carter didn't sound elegant enough for this high-class establishment.'

But Jacob misses all the irony. 'You sing here? That's wonderful! Then you're really an actress?'

'It says so on the program.'

'But that's great! That's what you always wanted to be, isn't it?'

'That's what I always wanted to be,' Sharon echoes drily. Then her concern for Jacob comes uppermost again. She asks how he came to leave the Carters'. Without any bitterness, he explains that he was fired a few days after she left the ranch. After that, he had a job over by Palmdale. But, as he shyly explains, he kept thinking about her and wondering where she was. Finally, he made up his mind to come to Los

Angeles. 'I felt sure we'd meet up sooner or later,' he adds simply.

Doc and Zacconi have been watching and listening to all this. Zacconi is obviously considering what use he can make of this unexpected meeting. His manner becomes benevolent in the extreme.

Innocently, Jacob goes on to say how pleased the professor and Miss Annie will be to hear that she has made good, and asks if they have already been to hear her sing. Sharon's reply makes it clear that she has been too proud to admit her failure to her father and aunt.

Zacconi now changes the subject by telling Sharon how he heard of Jacob's exploits as a healer, and adds that he and Doc have been trying to persuade Jacob to go into partnership with them.

Sharon doesn't like the sound of this at all. 'You ought to go right back to the desert,' she tells Jacob. 'This is no place for you.'

This doesn't suit Zacconi. Concealing his annoyance under an oily smile, he interrupts Sharon to ask her what she wanted to see him about. Sharon hesitates, mutters that it's nothing. Some other time will do. But Zacconi, sensing an advantage, insists that there's no time like the present. If it's a private matter, they can step outside for a moment. His manner fairly drips with sweetness.

He and Sharon step out of the office into a narrow alleyway behind the stage. Snatches of dialogue and music, mingled with applause, are heard from the other side of the stage scenery.

39

'Lou,' says Sharon, with the frankness of old and not too friendly acquaintance, 'I'm broke. Can I have ten bucks out of next week's check? You don't have to put on an act, either. Just yes or no.'

'But of course, my dear. Of course.' Zacconi pulls out his billfold and counts off the bills. But when Sharon puts out her hand for them, he stops her.

'Just a moment. From what you said just now, I got the impression that maybe you didn't like to work for me. I hope I was wrong?'

'What do *you* think?' she asks, sarcastically.

'You shouldn't be that way. A smart girl like you. Why, I was just getting ready to offer you a raise. Five bucks a week. What do you say?'

'Thank you *so* much, Mr Zacconi . . . Who do you want murdered?'

Zacconi laughs, rather too heartily. 'Listen, baby, you and me are old friends. I didn't like the way you talked to that Ericson kid. It wasn't nice. What's wrong with this outfit anyway? You've got to make him come in with us. For his own good – and yours.'

'And suppose I won't?' Sharon asks, defiantly.

Zacconi shrugs his shoulders. 'I can get all the singers I want. In this city they're a dime a dozen.'

'I see . . . So that's the way it is.'

'That's the way it is, baby. Now are you going to be reasonable, or aren't you?'

'Listen, Lou. You win. But let me tell you something. If I find you double-crossing Jacob, God help you. Because then I won't care what I do to you. Understand?'

Zacconi smiles easily. 'Who talked about double-crossing? This is just a business deal. Strictly on the level.'

'It had better be.'

'Say – you like that kid an awful lot, don't you?'

'Never mind about that. You and Doc aren't fit to shine his shoes, that's all.'

Zacconi grins. The whole thing has worked out just the way he wanted it. 'Sensible girl,' he tells Sharon approvingly. He hands her the bills and gives her a little pat on the fanny. They go back into the office where Doc has been treating Jacob to some of his ethical sentiments and five-dollar words.

'I've been thinking things over,' Zacconi tells Jacob. 'Maybe you're right about the theater. We want to keep this thing refined. Let's forget about it – for the present. Now are you coming in with us? What do you say?'

Jacob, in his perplexity, turns to Sharon.

'Do you think I should?' he asks.

'Do you *want* to?' Sharon counterquestions. She wants to dodge the responsibility.

'I'll do whatever you say.'

'And she says yes!' Zacconi adds confidently, with a wink at Doc.

'Do you, Sharon?' Jacob insists.

Slowly, unwillingly, Sharon nods her head.

'All right, then . . .' says Jacob doubtfully.

The words aren't out of his mouth before Zacconi has picked up the already prepared contract from the desk and offered it to Jacob with his fountain pen.

'Believe me, kid,' he says, as he pats Jacob on the back, 'you won't regret this. No, sir! You and me and Doc are going places!'

PART THREE

A few months have elapsed. Dressed in incongruous city clothes, in which he looks awkward and feels uncomfortable, Jacob is engaged in spending his pocket money where he always spends it – at the pet shop. Surrounded by cages full of mammals, birds, and reptiles, Jacob is talking to the old proprietor and his motherly wife about the charms and foibles of a pet lemur, which has taken his fancy.

He decides to buy it and is just paying for it when Sharon enters the shop.

'I might have known you'd be here,' she exclaims in the reproachful tone of a wife who has just located her husband in his favorite saloon. (And, in effect, this is precisely what, for Jacob, the pet shop is – the place where he spends his money and wastes the time he ought to be devoting to business.)

Sheepishly, Jacob tries to excuse himself.

'It's a real bargain,' he says, pointing to the lemur. 'Only twenty-five dollars.'

'But where will you keep it?' Sharon asks.

'Oh, there'll always be room,' Jacob answers, optimistically.

'Lou will be mad at you,' she warns.

Jacob grins mischievously like a naughty child. To change the subject, he pulls a little box out of his pocket, opens it, and produces a necklace of amber beads.

'I thought they'd match your hair,' he says as he hands them to her.

Sharon is touched, but feels she has to scold him for wasting his money. And, besides, there are other things she has to talk to him about. Why didn't he come back to the office after lunch? There are four or five patients waiting for an interview. Doc has sent her out to look for him.

'I was just on my way back,' Jacob mutters.

'Two and a half hours late!'

'But what's the good of my trying to cure people when I don't feel like it? It doesn't work then. I can't force it. You know I can't do it every day.'

Of course, Sharon agrees soothingly. But he can be there, at the office. He can talk to the people and make sure they come back for another treatment.

He shakes his head. 'I don't like to do it. I'm no salesman.'

'Like it or not, you signed a contract.' And, taking him by the arm, she leads him out, half repentant, half sullen, into the street. Carrying the lemur on his shoulder, he walks along beside her back to the office.

The Psycho-Magnetic Medical Center is located in a two-story house on a large thoroughfare. Doc Waldo receives the patients on the ground floor and goes

46

through an elaborate act to prepare them for their meeting with Jacob.

Sharon hands Jacob over to Doc's nurse and takes her leave, for she has to hurry back to the theater to get ready for the first show. The nurse whispers to Jacob that the doctor is hopping mad and hurries him through the waiting room (where the patients react in some surprise to the lemur) and into his office.

Jacob goes into a back room filled with more or less exotic pets, pops the lemur into a cage, and, coming back, slips on the professional white smock which is supposed to make him look ethical and scientific.

Then he goes through into Waldo's office, where he finds Doc doing his stuff with a stout middle-aged lady of most unprepossessing appearance. Stethoscope, blood-pressure recorder, and fluoroscope are all brought into play. Then there is a stream of medical jargon and a sales talk about the unique service offered by the Psycho-Magnetic Medical Center – a combination of the most advanced scientific therapy with magnetic treatment by one who is perhaps the greatest natural healer of our times, Mr Ericson – who has unfortunately been prevented from getting back to the office before this, on account of a pressing out-of-town call for his services. But now, Doc adds significantly, Mr Ericson will make up for lost time and give Mrs Kugelman the first of her magnetic treatments without further delay.

But instead of getting down to work as he should, Jacob asks the doctor to step into his office for a moment.

Doc follows him, and when the door is closed, Jacob tells him that he really can't do anything with this woman. There is something about her that he doesn't like. 'I can't explain. She just isn't on the level.'

'But she's the richest client we've had,' Waldo protests. And besides, he goes on to point out, Mrs Kugelman hasn't got a thing wrong with her. She's had too much leisure to think about herself, that's all. Just a case for suggestion. There is a good chance of making a spectacular 'cure'.

This is exactly what Jacob has sensed. And he stubbornly refuses. There's something bad about her, he repeats; and he's never been able to do anything for bad people.

Doc raves and rants, but Jacob can't be moved.

'I'll take that little crippled kid that's out there in the waiting room. And I'll try what I can do for the old man, and the woman there. But not Mrs Kugelman.'

Defeated, Waldo has to go back and explain diplomatically to his patient that Mr Ericson has made previous appointments and can't treat her today.

A couple of hours later Jacob has finished work and is amusing himself with his pets, when the door bursts open and in rushes Zacconi, followed by Doc.

'What's this Doc's been telling me?' Zacconi begins angrily.

The lemur, which seems to have a good nose for moral values, begins to chatter menacingly as Zacconi approaches, and only Jacob's timely intervention saves him from being bitten. This shock to his nerves sends Zacconi right up into the air. His pent-up irritation bursts out in paroxysms of fury, and he starts to yell. All Jacob's shortcomings are hurled at his head. His unreliability (he's worse than all the female wrestlers put together), the way he neglects his work, his failure to cure everybody who comes to him.

Jacob answers mildly that he has never claimed to be able to cure everybody; but Lou cuts him short.

'What do you think I'd do with a juggler who said he couldn't catch the ball every time?' he asks. 'I'd boot him out. And that's what I'm going to do with you, Ericson, if you go on like this.'

With exasperating calm and good humor, Jacob replies that he wouldn't at all mind being booted out. He's strong, he's not afraid of hard work. There will always be plenty of jobs waiting for him in the lumberyard here in the city or out on some ranch in the desert. In fact, if it wasn't for Sharon, he'd have cleared out long before this.

The mention of Sharon's name only makes Zacconi madder. He declares that he's known all along that she was responsible for all Jacob's moods. For Jacob's sake, he's taken more from that dame than he'd take from a top-flight opera star. But this is the end. From now on, both of them are going to toe the line, or else. Who in hell does she think she is – a cheap little so-and-so. He'll show her.

'Listen,' says Jacob, unexpectedly roused, 'you'd better leave Sharon alone. You'd better, that's all.'

His slowly aroused anger is so formidable that Zacconi quails before him. Zacconi would dearly love to take a poke at Jacob, but he doesn't dare. His eyes look daggers.

'Now get out of here,' Jacob tells him. 'And remember what I said about Sharon. Fire me if you want to. But leave her alone.'

Zacconi and Doc slink out, followed by the lemur's mocking chatter.

Jacob sits down heavily in a chair. He looks thoroughly disgusted with his surroundings.

Next morning Jacob and Sharon are strolling around the zoo in the park. Jacob is in a lively mood – a complete contrast to the morose young man we just saw in Doc's office. Some kids are looking at the animals, and Jacob talks to them. His stories about the different beasts show really shrewd psychological observation and surprising humor. This is something he understands, and once again, as always when Jacob is on his own ground, we get the impression that this is no clumsy country boy, but a mature, sensitive person who has looked deeply into life and can make it seem interesting and exciting. Sharon's face, as he talks, shows that she is thinking the same thing. Her eyes shine with pleasure and admiration.

Presently they leave the cages and stroll out into the park, where they sit down under a tree.

'Jacob . . .' says Sharon after a pause, during which she evidently comes to a decision, 'you know, when you're out here — just us two alone like this — you seem like a different person.'

Jacob grins. 'Well, I guess I am.'

'You hate that office — and working with Lou and Doc — don't you?'

He looks away from her quickly.

'It's not so bad,' he mutters.

'It's awful,' says Sharon emphatically. 'You know it is. You don't belong there at all.'

Jacob says nothing.

'And I got you into it,' she continues, full of self-reproach. 'It was all my fault.'

Still he doesn't answer.

'Listen, Jacob. Why don't you clear out? Why don't you go back where you belong?'

Jacob looks at her with a sudden, childish eagerness which shows how much he likes the idea.

'You think I should?'

'Sure. What's stopping you?'

Something seems to be bothering him. Presently he says: 'The contract!'

Sharon laughs, hearing her own words thrown back at her. 'Oh, we'll beat that! In the first place, it isn't fair. Maybe if it goes into court, the judge'll throw it out. And even if he doesn't, what can they do to you? Take away what you earned? What do you care? There's plenty of work. Tell you not to cure people for money? You don't want to, anyway . . . Besides, you could go to another state.'

Jacob thinks this over. 'There's – there's another reason,' he finally admits.

'What's that?' Sharon knows all right, but she wants to hear him say it.

Jacob looks away. 'You.'

Sharon's eyes shine. She touches his sleeve. 'I'd come with you, Jacob. That is – if you want me.'

Jacob's face lights up. He can hardly believe it. 'You would?'

Sharon nods slowly, smiling.

'But – what about your career?'

Sharon laughs rather bitterly. 'My career! You don't mean the Art Theater, by any chance?'

'But, Sharon – one day you'll get a break. I know it. You can't stop now. I couldn't ask you to.'

'That's my worry, Jacob. Not yours.'

'I know. Only –' Jacob breaks off. He utters a boyish laugh of delight. 'You really like me – that much?'

'A lot more than that much,' says Sharon, smiling at him tenderly.

He moves forward as if to kiss her. But something stops him. Perhaps he still can't quite believe it's true. His face is radiant. Sharon gently presses his hand. Then she rises to her feet, pulling him up.

'Let's go tell them,' she says.

Hand in hand, they walk away down the hill.

Meanwhile, at the office, Lou and Doc are sitting together, planning a new deal. Jacob is to be made to toe the line. From next week on, Zacconi is going to insist that he appear on the stage of the Art Theater. They've fooled around long enough. Zacconi repeats this several times, as if to reassure himself. We see that he is actually a bit scared of Jacob and doesn't relish having to tell him. This makes him extra venomous.

The nurse comes in to announce that there is a colored man in the lobby who particularly wants to have a word with Mr Ericson.

'Why did you ever let him in?' Doc asks impatiently. 'You know I won't have niggers in this office, lowering the tone of the place.'

The nurse excuses herself by saying that he was very insistent, said it was a matter of life and death.

'Throw him out!' exclaims Zacconi impatiently.

The nurse goes out, but apparently she isn't successful, because we hear the sound of voices approaching the door, and she reenters, followed by the Negro we have already seen in Reverend Wood's church. His name is George Hamilton. He is a very pleasant-spoken man, with great good humor and smiling persistence, which bears down all opposition. Zacconi jumps to his feet with an exclamation of rage. The nurse shrugs her shoulders.

George Hamilton starts right in to explain. He hasn't come for himself but for his employer, Mr Medwin.

At the name, both Lou and the Doc prick up their ears.

'You don't mean Earl C. Medwin?' Zacconi asks, excitedly.

53

Yes, that is just exactly who George does mean. George is chauffeur at the Medwins' home. Young Mr Medwin, son of the late oil millionaire, is a very sick man. Always been sick. With his heart. It gets worse and worse. Mrs Medwin, that's his mother, has tried all kinds of doctors and cures, but nothing seems to do any good. When Mr Ericson cured George's little niece, George got the idea that maybe he could help the young master, too. George is evidently very fond of his employer.

At this moment, Jacob and Sharon make their appearance. Jacob recognizes George and shakes his hand warmly. Doc and Lou excitedly explain the situation. This unexpected windfall has made them more than cordial toward Jacob. It's a wonderful chance. Doc gives orders that he will see no patients today.

'Let's get going,' says Zacconi.

Sharon looks at Jacob. Now is their chance to speak.

'We've got something to tell you, Lou,' she says.

'Fine!' says Lou, who even feels kindly toward Sharon now. 'I'll be glad to hear about it – later. We can't keep Mr Medwin waiting.'

Jacob looks at Sharon helplessly.

'I'd better go, I guess,' he tells her. 'If he's a friend of George's.'

Sharon nods. After all, their settlement with Lou and Doc can wait. George leads the way down to the car. The lovers squeeze hands warmly. Then Jacob turns to follow the others. Sharon looks after him lovingly, but with slight misgivings.

PART FOUR

In the Medwins' big limousine on the way out to Beverly Hills, George Hamilton further explains the situation to Zacconi, Doc, and Jacob. Young Mr Earl is being attended by two doctors, one of them a very distinguished specialist from the East. Naturally, they wouldn't approve of healers. They think they're all fakes. Ordinarily, Mr Ericson would never be allowed inside the house if the doctors and Mrs Medwin knew what he had come for. But George has talked to Mr Earl and has sold him on the idea. They have been waiting their chance for weeks. Today the doctors and Mrs Medwin have gone out. There is nobody at home but the staff, so Mr Ericson can be smuggled upstairs to the sick man's room. George evidently enjoys this little conspiracy.

The Medwin home is an impressive Spanish–style mansion, standing in beautiful grounds. The car stops at the servants' entrance, and George hurries the three visitors into the house. There is a whispered conversation between George and the colored cook, who explains that the coast is clear. The English butler, a formidable obstacle, is asleep in his room. One of the colored maids, also in the plot, has offered to keep an eye on Mr Earl, and the day nurse has taken the opportunity to go out and do some shopping. We get the impression that all the Medwins' colored staff are in a benevolent conspiracy against the doctors and Mrs Medwin, and on behalf of Jacob, of whom they approve in advance because of what he did for George's little niece.

Earl is a young man of twenty-three, still quite a boy in appearance. He is smallish, slight, and strikingly handsome in a weak and faintly vicious way. One sees the marks of the chronic invalid in his petulance, boredom, and capacity for self-pity. He is a spoiled egotist, but he is attractive, and has an appealing, weak, boyish charm. His enormous, inherited fortune he takes as a matter of course. There is nothing material he can't buy, and so everything bores him. He is like a child surrounded by expensive toys which are no longer amusing. Shut up in his nursery-sickroom, he is appallingly ignorant of the simplest realities of everyday life.

Since childhood, he has suffered from a heart ailment, mitral stenosis, which has subjected him to painful and alarming attacks; but his real sickness is psychological – the terrible, gnawing fear of the heart patient. He is haunted by the dread of death. And this condition has been intensified by the kind of life his mother has made him live, coddled and protected, always thinking and worrying about himself. Part of him submits to this babying and clings to any form of protection; part of him hates it, is dissatisfied, loathes his own weakness and longs for freedom.

Such is the man into whose presence the three visitors are now introduced. In their eagerness to make a good impression, and at the same time to exploit the financial possibilities of the situation, Zacconi and Doc very nearly spoil everything. Doc leads off with a flowery speech about his young friend Ericson – the simple, untutored child of nature whom he, the man of science, has undertaken to help and guide. Then Lou breaks in with a recital of his own claims to consideration – the financial support, the enormous sacrifices he has made, because of his faith in Jacob and his longing to benefit humanity. All he asks, he says, is to cover his expenses.

Earl listens to them for a moment in bewilderment, then he turns petulantly to George.

'Which one's the healer?' he asks. 'You know I can't have a lot of people in the room at once. It tires me. Send the others away.'

And George, with the greatest firmness and good humor, bustles Doc and Lou out of the room. Jacob is alone with the young millionaire.

There couldn't be more of a contrast between the two. Beside Earl, Jacob seems almost like a member of an older generation, a grown man with a kid. Also, he looks enormously big and strong in comparison with the slightly built young invalid.

Earl is looking at him searchingly – as if studying his face for some sign of reassurance, of support. This boy has been disappointed so often in those who said they could help him.

'You know,' he says at last, 'you aren't anything like I expected . . . I thought you'd be much older.' He pauses, still considering Jacob. His fine eyes are very expressive; they suggest acute anxiety, mingled with a certain mocking hostility.

'What did George tell you about me?' he asks abruptly.

'Not very much. There wasn't time.'

'I suppose he told you' – Earl's hostility comes uppermost – 'that I'm a millionaire?'

'Yes, he did,' Jacob answers simply.

'I suppose he told you that there isn't anything Mother wouldn't do for you, and him – if you could cure me?'

'No, he didn't say that. He just wants you to get well. He's fond of you.'

Earl smiles ironically. 'Are your two friends . . . just fond of me?'

Jacob has to laugh at this. 'Well, no – not exactly.'

Earl laughs too. 'Say, where in the world did you dig up those two cheap crooks?'

Simply and briefly, Jacob tells the story of his association with Doc and Lou. He tells about his life in the desert and, blushingly, he tells about Sharon.

His tale makes a great impression upon Earl. He has never heard anything like this before. Jacob's account of his adventures touches and intrigues him; he seems to be getting a glimpse into another world. His tone of suspicion and hostility changes to one of friendliness, and he begins to question Jacob about his healing powers.

Jacob answers in his usual modest way, making no sweeping claims, admitting to failures, protesting that the power isn't under his control but seems to come from outside and to use him only as its instrument.

'Do you think you can cure me?' Earl asks, after a long pause.

'I don't know. I can try,' says Jacob. Then he asks, with his characteristic directness, 'Do you *want* to be cured?'

Earl stares at him. Nobody has ever asked him this question before.

'There are folks that don't,' Jacob tells him. 'I can always tell when I start to work on them. I can feel it. They *think* they want to get well, but they don't, inside. You can feel them holding on to their sickness. They know it, and they've gotten used to it, and they don't know what they'll do without it. That scares them.'

Earl is silent, thinking this over.

'Have you ever thought,' Jacob continues, 'what you'd do if you were well?'

'What else do you suppose I think about?' Earl's tone is bitter.

'And what would you do?'

'Why, I'd – I'd go around, enjoy life, have myself a good time – like all the other fellows . . .'

Jacob shakes his head, smiling gently. 'It isn't quite

that simple. Life looks a lot different when you're standing on your own two feet. Even if you *are* a millionaire.'

Earl smiles, too. 'I guess you're right . . . But I'd take my chance on that.'

'Fine!' Jacob nods encouragingly. 'Now remember, you've got to help me all you can. We've got to do this together.'

Earl responds, for a moment, to this mood of encouragement. Then his habitual depression and weakness get the upper hand.

'You know what's wrong with me, don't you?' he asks.

'Something with your heart.'

'Something with my heart,' Earl repeats, and gives a tortured little laugh. All at once he turns sharply toward the long French window which opens on the balcony outside his room.

'Go and draw that curtain,' he orders in a peremptory whisper.

Jacob does as he is told. After a silence, the sick man speaks again, 'I suppose you were in the war?'

Jacob nods affirmatively.

'What was the worst part of it?'

Jacob considers. 'The noise, I guess.'

'The noise? But I'd have thought that would have kept you from thinking about things . . . It's the silence that gets me. Listening for what's coming after you in the silence.'

He shudders. His face twitches. To calm himself, he takes a sip of water from the glass standing on the bed table. Jacob watches him with an expression of profound compassion.

Then he pulls a chair up close to the bed, sits down, and lays a hand on the sick man's chest.

'Try and let go,' he says. 'You're all tied up. I can feel it.' He passes his hand over Earl's heart. 'It's like you were hanging on to yourself – gripping yourself so hard that the blood can't pass through. You're scared, and you want to hold on to something, but it's yourself you've gotten hold of, and you're choking off your own life. There's nothing to be scared of. Let go, can't you? Let go.'

He goes on passing his hands over Earl's body for a little while, then smiles and nods encouragingly.

'That's better. That's much better.'

His hands go back to the heart and remain there. 'Just like a man that's drowning,' he murmurs to himself. 'He grabs hold of something he thinks'll save him. But it's his own throat. He's choking himself.'

His hands move, gently stroking the heart, again and again.

'Let go,' he keeps repeating. 'Let go. I don't want you to hang on to yourself. I want you to let go. I want you to let yourself get well.'

Earl's strained, nervous tension relaxes; he closes his eyes; his breathing becomes slower and fuller; he lets himself sink back more comfortably into the pillows.

There is a long silence. Then Jacob withdraws his hands and sits back in his chair.

Suddenly, Earl raises himself in the bed. There is a look of incredulity on his face as he whispers:

'I believe . . . I'm better.'

Then, as if to confirm for himself what he cannot yet fully accept, he turns toward the window.

'The curtain – pull it back again.'

Jacob gets up and draws it back. Intently, Earl stares out at the balcony. His expression of doubt changes to one of amazed delight.

'It's gone!' he says at last.

'What's gone?' Jacob asks.

Earl looks at him, hesitates for a moment, then speaks. For weeks now, he confides, he has been obsessed by the feeling, the conviction, that there's something there, on the balcony – something that peers through the window at him when he isn't looking; that comes into the room when he's asleep and stands by the bed and looks at him, waiting, waiting . . . He shudders, and glances once more apprehensively at the window, still haunted by that fear of death which has been torturing him. Then his face clears. There is nothing there.

'It's gone!' he repeats, almost ecstatically.

'That's because you let it go,' Jacob tells him.

'Yes,' Earl agrees eagerly, 'that's true . . . I know what you mean now. You said I had to help you. I think I can. When you put your hands on me just now, I saw it quite clearly for a minute. I saw how I had to let go. I *knew* I could let go . . . It was the darnedest feeling . . . I never knew how to do that, before. Never in my whole life . . .'

Jacob smiles wisely. To calm Earl down a little, he begins to talk about himself. He tells Earl how he also used to get tense and worried when he first came home from the war. What cured him was being with animals and seeing how they acted. They accept what comes. They don't argue and philosophize about the future. For them, there is nothing but the present moment. He tells Earl about his pets. Earl wants to see them. He has never had any pets of his own, because his mother doesn't like them, and they have been considered unsanitary to have around a sickroom.

'There's so much I've got to learn,' he says reflectively and with a newly found humility. Then with sudden anxiety, he adds, 'You'll stick around, won't you, Jacob? I need you now. More than I've ever needed anyone, I guess . . . I can't do this by myself. I know that. I've got to have you with me all the time, showing me how. If you leave me now – it'd be worse than if you'd never come at all. You won't leave me, will you?'

'I won't leave you,' Jacob promises, 'as long as you need me.'

'And that'll be an awful long time,' says Earl, smiling happily in his new sense of security.

But now voices are heard outside the door in excited and angry-sounding conversation.

In sweeps Mrs Medwin, Earl's mother, followed by

two doctors – Dr Rowan, the family physician, and Dr Krebs, the big specialist from the East, who has been called in for consultation. Behind them, extremely voluble, follow Zacconi and Doc.

Mrs Medwin, a fragile-looking little woman, whose petite good looks conceal the soul of a velvet-handed despot, makes straight for the bed, disregarding Jacob completely.

'My darling!' she wails. 'What have they been doing to you?'

Earl, very much discomfited, vainly tries to calm her down.

'Why, Mother, I'm all right. Jacob and I have been having a talk . . . Mother, this is Mr Ericson . . .'

But Mrs Medwin acknowledges Jacob's presence with the merest nod. Turning to her son, she continues: 'It's all my fault, darling. I should never leave you. Not for a moment . . . Oh dear, is there nobody in this house I can trust?'

'But, Mother –'

'Must I do everything? Must I be everywhere at once? Can't I ask for the very least bit of loyalty from anyone? It's like being stabbed in the back . . . I come home, and what do I find? These dreadful people –'

Indignant protests from Zacconi and Doc.

'It's all George's fault,' Mrs Medwin continues, her beautiful eyes liquid with reproach. 'And I trusted him implicitly. Well – he leaves at once. I won't have him in the house another minute.'

For two hours the battle rages, upstairs and down. The two doctors are mortally offended. Dr Krebs is ready to go back east at once. Dr Rowan feels that he must retire from the case. Waldo, vehemently protesting at being treated as a crooked quack, claims professional status and the rights of a colleague. The two physicians brush him off as though he were some kind of evil-smelling centipede. The day nurse, accused of being a deserter, is reduced to tears. The staff are fired in a body, and later rehired, as Mrs Medwin slowly calms down.

At length peace, or at any rate an armistice, is established. Mrs Medwin finds, to her tearful dismay, that Earl is absolutely firm in his determination to keep Jacob at his side. For the first time, he seems to be taking his place as master of the house, and there is nothing she can do to oppose him. Jacob is to stay right here. George is not to lose his job. What the others do, or don't do, Earl doesn't care.

So Krebs and Rowan are pacified, with compliments and feminine flattery, such as Mrs Medwin knows only too well how to apply. Zacconi and Doc are hurried off the premises, like blackmailers, squabbling over the enormous check which Mrs Medwin has angrily thrust into their hands, with the threat of legal action if they ever dare to show their faces around the house again. As for Jacob, he is unwillingly given the blue guest room. George is to fetch his few belongings from the Psycho-Magnetic Medical Center.

Earl further amazes the household by announcing that

he is coming downstairs to dinner. The two doctors at first forbid this absolutely, but Earl is so determined that they unwillingly agree, lest he should further excite himself and bring on another heart attack. So, with infinite precautions, and with many blankets and much anxious coddling, Earl is carried downstairs.

The atmosphere during the meal is several degrees below freezing point. Mrs Medwin, outwardly sweet – she knows how to make the best of a strategic withdrawal – has an eagle eye on Jacob's table manners. The English butler regards Jacob's ill-cut clothes with an expression of resignation and aesthetic pain. The doctors are coldly silent.

But Jacob's disarming friendliness disregards all this, and Earl, delighted with his new friend, laughs and jokes, doing his best to draw his mother into the conversation.

'Gee,' he exclaims, 'I haven't had so much fun in years!'

And the pathetic thing is that he is obviously speaking the literal truth.

PART FIVE

Less than two weeks have passed, but great changes have taken place at the Medwins'.

Earl is out in the garden – not in a wheelchair, either; but sitting on the lawn, fully dressed, laughing and playing with Jacob's lemur and the other pets. The elegant, formal flower beds are overrun with animals. We hardly recognize the petulant, scared invalid of the earlier scene. Earl appears in every way to be a normal young man, except that his overflowing gaiety and high spirits make him seem younger than his age. Everything delights him: the sunshine, the flowers, the trees, the blue sky overhead. He is enjoying being alive, in a way that very few adults ever do, unless they have just been released from a sickbed or a prison. The simplest sounds and sights and sensations are new to him, and still seem astonishingly beautiful.

Jacob, of course, is with him. They are seldom separated. If Jacob goes away, even for a few minutes, Earl gets uneasy. It is only then that we become aware of his weakness and utter dependence upon the older man. All his strength, all his assurance, is drawn from Jacob. He hasn't yet reached the point at which he can stand alone.

71

The Medwins' staff react strongly to the new conditions. The servants sing at their work, George is one big grin from ear to ear, the younger girls are quite stuck on Mr Earl. Everybody begins to notice how good-looking and attractive he is. And everybody is fond of Jacob. The gardener, finding his precious flowers destroyed by the animals, doesn't mind a bit. Even the butler has thawed out and makes British jokes.

Earl himself is charming to everybody. He can afford to be, now that he feels so happy. He has begun to take a great interest in the people who work for him and to inquire into their family histories and problems. He asks George to bring his little niece to the house, along with the cook's children.

The tableau in the garden is watched by Mrs Medwin and Dr Krebs. Dr Krebs is just about to leave for the East, to attend other, more urgent cases. Does he really think Earl is cured? Mrs Medwin asks.

The great specialist shrugs his shoulders. 'Cured' isn't a word one can use in these cases. Certainly there has been an improvement, which may or may not be sustained. A great deal depends on the psychological factor – he indicates Jacob – and that is quite unpredictable. On the whole, although he doesn't exactly say so, he is obviously pessimistic. Any time he is needed, Dr Krebs assures Mrs Medwin, he will drop everything and fly out to the Coast within twenty-four hours. In the meantime, he advises extreme caution and warns against overoptimism. Earl is still to be regarded as a sick man. Tactfully, Dr Krebs insinuates that he has seen a good deal of these so-called 'faith cures'. They often achieve remarkable temporary results, but these are merely due to a psychological shot in the arm, which draws on the patient's reserve energy. When this is exhausted – well, one can only hope there won't be a really serious relapse.

Mrs Medwin herself is somewhat confused in her feelings. There is no need to warn her not to be optimistic; her whole life is spent in a vortex of anxieties and fears, which she has unconsciously transmitted to her son. Still, she can't altogether disregard the evidence of her own eyes. Earl is transformed; he is up and about, doing things which would have seemed like suicide only two weeks ago. And she assures her son over and over again, with the most emotional sweetness, how happy she is to see it.

But is she really happy? Subconsciously, she is not; though she would never admit this, even to herself. All her mother love, on which she prides herself above everything else, is really a will to power. As long as Earl was helpless, he was hers, her own baby, her victim, her possession. Now she feels that he is passing out of her power. She knows better than anyone else that the new, revitalized Earl won't be content for long just to admire the flowers, and enjoy the sunshine, and play with the animals. He will want to go his own way, and whatever that way is, it will lead him out into the world. Inevitably, she will lose him.

She is fiercely jealous of Jacob, on whom Earl now

73

depends far more than he ever depended upon herself. Yet, just because Jacob is the enemy, her instinct advises her to make terms with him until the day comes when she can get rid of him altogether.

So she is very sweet to Jacob, complimenting him and flattering him in every possible way, but watching all the time for some clue to a hidden weakness in his character which she can use for her own purposes.

Jacob is bewildered by this complete change of attitude on the part of Mrs Medwin, but his own honesty of motive protects him against it. He doesn't seem to want money, she finds. And when she hints that Earl mustn't be allowed to depend upon him too much – the darling boy is *so* impressionable – Jacob disconcerts her by agreeing. He himself will be glad to leave the moment she feels that Earl can get along without him.

With Earl, she employs the same tactics. She praises Jacob to the skies; such a charming boy, so innocent, so unsophisticated, so completely without any guile. And so completely without any culture, any education, she contrives to hint.

But Earl, who knows his mother's every intonation, sees right through this diplomacy. 'You don't like him,' he tells her bluntly. 'And you needn't pretend that you do. You're jealous of him because you want to boss me around the way you always have. Well, listen – he's the first friend I've ever had in my life, and I'm going to keep him, no matter what.'

Earl is really angry. Mrs Medwin, seeing that she has

gone too far, takes refuge in tears. 'As if I ever begrudged you anything, darling, from the day you were born. Why, I'd give my life if it would make you happy! If you don't want me anymore, I'll go away from here altogether. I'd do anything in the world to please you.'

This is too much for Earl, who has a soft, weakly affectionate nature. Very much distressed, he takes back everything he has said. He didn't really mean it. He can't bear to see his mother cry. He loves her, she knows that. He realizes how much she's always done for him; what sacrifices she has made. Nevertheless, it is plain that he isn't ready to give up Jacob, either.

'Why do we have to fight,' he asks with innocent egotism, 'just when I'm so happy?'

So Mrs Medwin retires, and gathers her strength for the next round.

Jacob, meanwhile, has been thinking constantly of Sharon. Earl's utter dependence has kept him a prisoner at the Medwins', despite all his attempts to escape even for a few hours. Now, however, he manages to beg an evening off and hurries down to Main Street.

When Sharon leaves the stage door of the Art Theater, Jacob is waiting.

Sharon greets him rather coldly. She has been feeling neglected. We learn that Jacob has tried to call her several times and that, after hearing his first excuses that he couldn't get away, she has refused to answer at all. Not having seen Earl, and knowing nothing of the peculiar circumstances at the Medwins', she very naturally finds it hard to believe that Jacob has really been unable to come and see her for two weeks.

Jacob, very much upset by her attitude, explains as best he can. Sharon soon forgives him. She admits that she has been jealous. She's been imagining things; wondering if, perhaps, Earl has a sister or a pretty little nurse . . . They laugh over her suspicions. Presently they are walking down the street arm in arm, like lovers.

But there is something on Jacob's mind. Before he left that evening, Earl made him promise as a condition of his few hours' freedom that he will bring Sharon to the house the next day. Earl is like his mother in this; he wants to take complete possession of the lives of everybody around him. He has heard Jacob talk so much about Sharon that he cannot bear to think of her as outside his orbit. As long as he doesn't know her, he feels that she is taking a part of Jacob away from him.

Sharon is unexpectedly unwilling. Some instinct warns her against having anything to do with the Medwins. She doesn't want to get involved with any more city people. She doesn't want Jacob to be involved. Now that she has made up her mind to abandon this life altogether, she is eager to take the final step – perhaps because, at the back of her mind, there is still a faint doubt, a slight regret.

'You and I don't belong in that crowd,' she tells Jacob. 'What's the use of being with rich people when you haven't any money? It only gives you ideas.'

Jacob is himself so completely immune to the lures

of wealth that he can't altogether understand her point of view. To him, Earl is still just a sick boy who needs him – it might just as easily have been one of the colored people at Reverend Wood's church. As a matter of fact, the grandeur of life at the Medwin home makes him uncomfortable. To stay there costs him a considerable sacrifice. But if Sharon came, it wouldn't be so bad. If he could see her, now and then, he wouldn't mind.

Sharon is alarmed at the vagueness of his 'now and then'. How much longer, she wants to know, does he figure on staying there? What about their plans? Has Jacob forgotten?

He assures her that he hasn't. He never forgets for a moment. Very soon, Earl won't need him anymore. Then he and Sharon can leave Los Angeles for good, and how wonderful that will be!

His warmth and sincerity have their effect. Sharon gives in. She agrees, if it will please him, to come out to the Medwins' the next day.

'But goodness knows,' she adds smiling, 'what Mr Medwin will think of your girlfriend. I haven't a decent thing to wear!'

Jacob has, of course, made no secret of Sharon's profession. And so Mrs Medwin prepares herself to confront a new enemy. A showgirl – in her house! Some cheap little gold digger, no doubt, who will try to get a foothold in high society by making a fool of Earl, the impressionable. She decides to freeze Sharon to death, right from the start.

But Sharon, when she appears, is a great surprise. Instead of the flaunting showgirl Mrs Medwin expected, there appears a charming young woman, simply but tastefully dressed, very quiet, very unassuming.

Mrs Medwin questions her, unobtrusively but expertly, during tea and is agreeably surprised to find that Sharon has a 'background' – her father is actually a university professor! Sharon is, naturally, very unwilling to talk about the Carters; but her reticence is approved by Mrs Medwin as an evidence of modesty.

Far from making eyes at Earl, she scarcely seems to notice him. It is obvious that she is very much in love with Jacob; and she further allays Mrs Medwin's fears by making it clear that her intention is to take him away from the Medwin home and Los Angeles as soon as possible. By the end of the afternoon, Mrs Medwin has come to regard the girl as a potential ally.

Earl is delighted with Sharon. His experience of girls has been necessarily limited to his nurses, and Mrs Medwin has been careful to pick the less attractive ones to attend her son. Earl is by nature a highly emotional and erotic type. But at present, in the first romantic phase of his convalescence, he hasn't begun to think of himself in relation to any particular girl. He is quite content to bask in the atmosphere of Sharon and Jacob's love for each other.

When Sharon has gone, he spends the evening talking

about her and congratulating Jacob on his happiness. Jacob listens with delight. Earl has, in fact, taken possession of their affair and regards it with a kind of wistful, brotherly pleasure. He even has schemes that Jacob and Sharon shall be married from the Medwin home. From now on, he declares, they are all going to be the greatest friends and see as much of each other as possible.

For some years, the Medwins have owned a beach house near Santa Monica, down on the ocean. It has hardly ever been used, but now Earl, who is at length getting a little tired of the garden, begins going down there with Jacob to spend the day in the sun. And Sharon, of course, is invited to come along too.

While Jacob goes for a run along the beach with the dogs, Earl gets the opportunity of talking to Sharon alone.

Naturally, they talk about Jacob. It is the only subject they have in common. Earl asks Sharon what she and Jacob plan to do when they are married. Sharon replies that she supposes they'll go and live somewhere out in the country, work, eventually buy a ranch, settle down, have kids, and stay there for the rest of their lives. Perhaps a note of slight wistfulness comes into her voice, and a tone of slight resignation. This isn't lost on Earl, who is extraordinarily sensitive and observant.

'And what about your singing?' he asks.

'Maybe the cows and the roosters will appreciate it,' says Sharon, with whom this is still a sore subject.

'You shouldn't talk that way,' Earl tells her. 'You ought to believe in yourself more.'

The sympathy of this good-looking boy is very agreeable to her. More so, perhaps, than she is ready to admit.

'I haven't had much encouragement,' she says with the old bitterness coming into her voice.

'Jacob believes in you,' Earl reminds her.

'Jacob . . .' Sharon smiles. 'That's different. That's only because I'm me. Besides, he doesn't know anything about music.'

'I believe in you,' says Earl softly and very seriously.

'You really do, Earl?' This is the first time that she has called him by his name. 'You wouldn't kid me?'

'You *know* I wouldn't . . . Why, you could do anything you wanted to. You could be a great singer. You've got a lovely voice . . . and lots of personality . . . and you're beautiful.'

Sharon laughs. Earl, in his own way, is as naïve as Jacob. But just the same she is pleased and flattered and excited; after all, he is a well-educated, cultured boy. His opinion must be worth something. He talks with such conviction. And he has such beautiful eyes.

'How do you know what you can do?' he continues, pressing his advantage. 'You haven't tried.'

'I've had my chance. I never got any place.'

'You call that a chance? Why, those bums on Main Street wouldn't know Mary Garden from a rooster.'

Sharon has to admit that this is true.

And then Earl unfolds his scheme. He has been thinking things over and he has it all figured out in advance. The man who owns the Star and Garter, one of Hollywood's most exclusive nightclubs, was an old friend of his father's. In fact, some of the Medwin millions went into backing him; Earl still owns shares in the place. This man would be only too glad of a chance to acknowledge his debt by doing Earl a favor. And, besides, this wouldn't really be a favor, because Earl would be helping his business by presenting him with a new star.

Sharon, of course, is thrilled and dazzled by the prospect. All her dormant ambition is aroused. To have one more chance – a real chance this time, of realizing those dreams of the old days on the Carter Ranch! Maybe Earl is right. Maybe she hasn't been fair to herself. Wasn't it just weakness which made her decide she could never be a singer? Hasn't she been too ready to accept defeat?

But then she hesitates. No, it's just a dream. She has made her decision. She loves Jacob, and the rest of her life is for him. When you want anything badly, you always have to make some sacrifices.

'But how do you know,' says Earl, 'that Jacob would be against it? I should think he'd be tickled to death.'

'I'd never even ask him,' says Sharon with decision. 'It wouldn't be fair.'

'Why not?'

'Well – suppose you're right. Suppose I did make good. It would be spoiling his whole life.'

81

'I don't see that at all. You could get married right away.'

'Can you imagine Jacob married to an actress? Hanging around my dressing room? Coming with me to parties? Why, he'd be miserable.'

'And wouldn't you be miserable,' asks Earl with a sudden touch of what is almost cruelty, 'milking cows and feeding chickens?'

Sharon looks quickly away from him. 'At least I'd be with Jacob,' she says at length.

'Throwing the garbage to the pigs,' Earl persists, sadistically teasing.

'If that's the way he wants it,' says Sharon firmly.

'But, Sharon, he *couldn't* want it. He couldn't want to make you unhappy . . . I know darn well I'd – I'd never ask you to do anything like that.'

They are on the verge of criticizing Jacob, but Sharon hardly realizes it.

'Earl,' she says gently, 'you just don't understand how it is . . . The girl you marry will probably want the same things you want.'

'If she didn't,' says Earl obstinately, 'I'd be the one to give way. A fellow has to make a girl happy.'

Sharon is silent. Mentally, she contrasts the two of them. Earl has been spoiled and petted, no doubt, but he seems so easy to get along with. Jacob, on the other hand, always appears so docile, and yet there is something unyielding and independent about him. He has always gone his own way. Perhaps that is why she loves him.

Earl is watching her reactions. He presses his advantage. 'Of course,' he continues, 'I could quite understand your going to live on the ranch one day – later on – when you'd had your career and everything. Then you'd know you hadn't missed anything. You wouldn't be unhappy then. You wouldn't have any regrets . . . Look here, why can't you two come to an agreement? You have your chance at the Star and Garter, and do the things you want to do. Then it will be Jacob's turn.'

'I couldn't ask him,' Sharon repeats with decision. 'It wouldn't be fair.'

'Do you think it's fair *not* to ask him? Suppose he got to know about this later? Wouldn't he feel like a heel?' Earl looks down the beach. Jacob is approaching. 'Suppose we let him decide?'

'Earl – you're not to say anything about it!'

'Why not?'

'Promise me you won't!' Sharon is greatly distressed. 'Promise!'

But Earl only laughs at her like a teasing little boy.

Jacob runs up.

'Sharon and I have been having a talk,' Earl tells him, his eyes sparkling with mischief. 'She's got something to tell you.'

'Earl!' exclaims Sharon reproachfully.

'What is it?' Jacob asks, smiling from the one to the other.

'Nothing – Earl was only joking.'

'Okay,' says Earl, 'if she won't tell you, I will . . .' And he describes his plan in glowing colors. Sharon weakly protests. Then she is silent.

'Well, what do you think of it?' Earl asks, when he has finished.

'Why,' says Jacob enthusiastically, 'I think it's just wonderful!'

'You see?' Earl turns triumphantly to Sharon.

'But, Jacob' – Sharon is anxious and a trifle disappointed – 'you mean you really don't mind?'

'Why should I mind?'

'Well, you know, it might – it might interfere with our plans just for a little, that is . . .'

'But, Sharon,' says Jacob innocently, 'it's what you've always wanted, isn't it?'

'Yes, but –'

'Well, then, I want you to do it.'

Sharon searches his face for some sign of disappointment. She can find none. If Jacob feels any more than he says, he doesn't show it. And already Sharon is sold on the idea. Her imagination is at work on all kinds of pictures of the wonderful future which suddenly seems to be opening out ahead of her.

As for Earl, he is delighted. Power-loving like his mother, he enjoys being able to intervene in the lives of his two friends. He feels like a kind of benevolent Providence.

'You two don't have to worry about a thing,' he tells them. 'Everything's going to be just the way you want it. Leave it all to me.'

★　　★　　★

84

Sure enough, less than a month later, Jacob and Earl are sitting at a ringside table in the Star and Garter Club, waiting for Sharon to make her debut.

For Sharon herself, it has been a hectic time: rehearsals, fittings, posing for publicity photographs, and more rehearsals. The two men have scarcely seen her. Jacob, no doubt, has thought about her constantly, from one day's end to another. But it is Earl who has remembered to pay her more tangible attentions – flowers every day, with little notes attached, and telephone calls. Jacob is not much good at telephoning, and it is Earl who has kept her informed of his various doings. In one way or another, Earl has contrived to keep his presence in Sharon's mind. After all, it is he to whom she owes this whole extraordinary adventure.

Jacob and Earl are both in tuxedos, new ones, just home from the tailor. Jacob's somehow doesn't suit him, despite its faultless cut. Whereas Earl – although he is wearing evening clothes for the first time in his life – seems perfectly at ease. Already, he is recognizing the nightclub as his spiritual home. His eyes greedily enjoy the scene; the lights, the dresses, the beautiful women. This is the world he has dreamed of on his sickbed, and now he is part of it.

The floor show begins. There are one or two preliminary numbers. Then it is Sharon's turn. She is the featured singer.

She gives quite an adequate performance. There is no spectacular failure. But somehow she doesn't put it

85

across. She is just a lovely girl with a nice voice, nothing more. The comments of the guests at the other tables are not too enthusiastic. Nobody is much impressed. One or two people know who Sharon is, and there are the usual, slightly malicious remarks. People look at Earl and whisper. They are surprised that the Medwin boy, so wealthy and good-looking, hasn't picked himself a more sensational girlfriend.

'What does he see in her?' the women wonder, somewhat enviously. And the unspoken question is added, 'What has she got that I haven't?' The men are more charitable. They, at least, admire Sharon's face and figure, but they don't see why she has to sing.

However, when Sharon has finished, there is sufficient applause. Most of it is contributed by Earl and Jacob. Jacob is the only person in the room who is quite unaware that Sharon hasn't had a sensational triumph.

Sharon comes over to their table and is congratulated. She herself is a little depressed. When Earl praises her, she shakes her head. 'They didn't like it,' she says despondently. 'I was lousy.'

'Nonsense,' Earl encourages her. 'You were a bit nervous, that's all. You'll be all right by tomorrow evening.'

Sharon isn't so sure, but his confidence gradually infects her. Maybe it *was* just nervousness. She isn't used to this kind of audience. She begins to cheer up.

Earl is at his best. She responds gratefully to his

high spirits. Very soon their table becomes the center of attention. All kinds of people come to speak to them – apparently to congratulate Sharon, but actually to have the excuse of introducing themselves to Earl.

The men have various business motives for wanting to be friendly to the young millionaire. The women are out to catch him, if they can. Earl enjoys this hugely. His vanity is aroused. He flirts and makes wisecracks; but his attention is always directed toward Sharon. In the presence of all these people, he treats her more and more as though she were what everybody thinks she is, his girlfriend. Jacob is practically ignored.

Noticing this, Earl sets himself to bring Jacob into the picture. But the way he does this is not altogether kind. Earl doesn't realize that he is being malicious toward Jacob. It is simply that he himself is excited, and that he has become so quickly a part of his surroundings that he now behaves and reacts like any other rich young man-about-town.

Without any conscious ill will, he makes fun of Jacob, exploiting his innocence and lack of sophistication, and thereby inviting everybody else to laugh at him. He gets Jacob to admit that he has never heard of any of the motion picture actresses who are present; and he quotes Jacob's naïve comments on the life of the nightclub so that they seem much more ridiculous than they really are.

Sharon realizes this and doesn't altogether like it. But

Earl's high spirits infect her, and she begins to adopt the same tone.

As for Jacob himself, he is unconscious of any cruelty in their humor – being quite incapable of cruelty himself. He smilingly reacts to Earl's jokes. In the midst of the laughter, he retains that curious natural dignity which never leaves him and which arises from his own honesty and simplicity. Sharon and Earl are rather like two small children laughing at an elephant.

But the noise and the lights and the talk make Jacob sleepy, and soon he begins to yawn. Why doesn't he go back home, Earl suggests; George can drive him. Earl and Sharon will follow in a taxi later.

Jacob immediately agrees. They are enjoying themselves; he isn't. It doesn't occur to him to be jealous.

As Jacob and George are driving home in the car, George asks if they had a good time and how Jacob liked the nightclub. Jacob answers quite humorously, describing it in his direct, unaffected way and making it clear that he was well aware of being out of place there.

Then he goes on to say how much Sharon and Earl are enjoying themselves, and he tells George about the success of Sharon's singing. He speaks with unselfish pleasure in her happiness, but it is possible to detect a slightly wistful note in his voice. Once more he has been made conscious of the great gulf which exists between Sharon and himself. They belong to different worlds.

This isn't lost on George. He is too tactful to express any sympathy, but we feel that a deep understanding is growing up between the two men. They have something fundamental in common. Both are simple and honest. And both, for different reasons, feel lonely and excluded.

George changes the subject, asking Jacob about the desert. He has always wanted to get away from the big city, into an atmosphere where racial and class distinctions don't count. Jacob describes the beauties of the Mojave and again we are aware how little he likes his present surroundings. When they reach the Medwin home, they say good night to each other like old friends.

Meanwhile, at the Star and Garter, Sharon and Earl are having the time of their lives. Instinctively, they feel much freer now that Jacob has left them. They are nearly the same age; and Sharon becomes younger and more lighthearted in Earl's company. Now that the floor show is over, she offers to teach him to dance. Earl proves to be an astonishingly apt pupil. These things come naturally to him.

In these days of Prohibition, the male guests bring their own liquor in hip-pocket flasks. The club provides setups of mineral water or ginger ale to mix with it; these are charged for at huge prices.

Earl, of course, has no flask of his own, but there are plenty of his new acquaintances who are ready to offer theirs. Sharon, becoming motherly for a moment, reminds him of his heart. Hadn't he better be careful?

But Earl laughs off her anxiety. His heart is as good as anybody's, nowadays. And besides, what the heck, you only live once. He is so confident that Sharon has to give way and join him in a drink. But her solicitude delights Earl. He gives her hand a squeeze and tells her she's the greatest girl in the world.

It is very late when they finally climb into a taxi to return home. Both have had several drinks and can't stop laughing. It was a wonderful evening, Earl declares. He didn't know anything could be so much fun. And this is just the beginning. There are going to be plenty more.

Suddenly, he takes Sharon in his arms and kisses her. She is startled and disengages herself.

'Earl, are you crazy?'

Earl laughs gaily. 'I guess I am – about you.'

But Sharon has had a nasty shock. She has allowed this situation to build itself up, throughout the evening, without thinking what it was leading to. Or maybe she didn't want to think. Certainly, she has been giving Earl every encouragement. It's just as much her fault as his.

She says, very seriously, 'Haven't you forgotten about Jacob? How'd you feel if he'd seen you just then?'

'But he didn't see,' Earl laughs. Then, with a change of tone, 'Be your age, baby. What's the harm in a little kiss?'

He is so exactly like a naughty little boy that Sharon begins to feel she has made too much fuss about a trifle. After all, she has been kissed before, plenty of times. The

Main Street Art Theater wasn't exactly a convent. And Earl is such a kid. She smiles at him.

Earl follows up his advantage by insisting on just one more kiss before they arrive at Sharon's hotel – 'to say good night.' After a lot of good-humored argument, Sharon kisses him on the cheek and firmly stops him when he impulsively tries to grab her and start something more drastic.

'I shan't come out with you again,' she tells him playfully, 'if you don't promise to be good.'

Sharon goes to bed that night with mixed feelings. She tries to feel that nothing serious has happened. She has had to handle much tougher propositions than Earl in the Main Street days. Tonight didn't really mean a thing. Nevertheless, when she thinks of Jacob, she feels guilty. Perhaps she'll tell him all about it tomorrow. Or perhaps she won't. He might not understand. Earl is a nice boy. Just a harmless kid. And so good-looking. And he's had a bad time. No wonder he wants some fun out of life now he's well. And I owe him so much, Sharon thinks, looking around her comfortable hotel bedroom and mentally contrasting it with the dreary Main Street room she used to share with another of the girls. Maybe, she thinks, I was unreasonable this evening. After all, Jacob will never know.

Earl also is restless that night. He arrives home in a state of great excitement – partly because of the scene with Sharon, partly because of the alcohol he has drunk – and when he gets into bed, he can't sleep. His heart begins acting up and a growing uneasiness comes over him. He begins glancing at the window. We realize that his old fears are returning. At length, he climbs out of bed; he is shaking with fright, yet trying hard to control himself. He goes to the window. Of course there is nothing there.

Reassured, he lies down again – and at last drops off into an uneasy doze.

Then he sits up in bed with a wild cry of panic. He fumbles desperately for the light switch and the bell which connects him with Jacob's bedroom.

A moment later, Jacob is beside him. Earl is gasping with fright.

'Jacob – I thought – I thought it was back again – outside the window.'

Jacob reassures him. There is nothing there. He can see for himself. 'We sent it away, didn't we?'

'Sure,' Earl agrees. 'We sent it away.'

But he is still uneasy. Jacob, watching his face with affectionate shrewdness, asks, 'What's bothering you, Earl? There *is* something. I can see it.'

Earl protests that there's nothing. He had a marvelous evening. We are aware of his evasiveness. Now, for the first time since they met, there is something he can't tell Jacob.

But gradually, under the soothing influence of Jacob's presence, he calms down. Soon he is peacefully asleep.

Jacob goes quietly out of the room.

★   ★   ★

Several weeks have passed. At the Medwin home, a party is in progress. It is a very different scene from the party at the nightclub. Today is Jacob's birthday. And Earl and Sharon – perhaps because they both feel rather guilty toward him – have combined to make it a success. Jacob has been asked what he would most like to do, and he has replied by inviting all the children of the staff to a birthday dinner.

The dark-skinned sons and daughters, nephews and nieces, of the colored help mingle with four or five white children and the two little granddaughters of the Cantonese laundryman. Mrs Medwin has retired to her bedroom, after giving the butler strict orders to lock up the silver and see that nothing is damaged or stolen. The children are making a tremendous amount of noise. Sharon and Earl join in the fun. Earl is as noisy as any of the kids. As for Jacob, he is enjoying himself hugely. Everything seems gay, harmless, and innocent.

After dinner, the children and the three grown-ups play hide-and-seek. Sharon hides in an upstairs room. Earl 'finds' her there. He has obviously been watching her and waiting for this chance.

'I wanted to give you this,' he tells her, taking something from his pocket. 'There's no reason why Jacob should have all the presents.'

It is a tiny wristwatch, set in diamonds.

Sharon gasps with delight. But she shakes her head. 'Earl – you know as well as I do I can't take it.'

'What's the matter? Don't you like it?'

'It's beautiful, but –'

'But what?'

'For goodness' sake, Earl,' exclaims Sharon, exasperated, 'don't pretend to be so innocent. Stop acting like a kid. We're grown-up people.'

'Okay,' says Earl, watching her with a peculiar smile. 'If that's the way you want it –' And he takes her in his arms. This time the embrace is passionate. Sharon visibly responds for a moment before she breaks free.

'I've got to get out of here,' she says, more to herself than to him. 'We can't go on like this.'

'Can't we?' Earl grins. 'You've said that before.'

'I thought you were Jacob's friend,' she says bitterly.

But Earl doesn't react. He is looking at her triumphantly, maliciously.

'I thought you were Jacob's girl.'

Sharon is almost in tears of vexation and guilt. 'You make me feel such a heel. I hate you sometimes.'

Earl's manner changes. 'Don't be that way, Sharon. Is it my fault if Jacob doesn't give you what you want?'

'Jacob's different –'

'Sure, he's different. Jacob wants to put you on a pedestal and admire you. I want to kiss you and hold you in my arms.'

'I'm in love with him, Earl. Don't forget that.'

'And you like kissing me. Don't forget that, either.'

Sharon can't deny it. 'We've got to stop seeing each other,' she tells him.

Earl smiles and says nothing. His silence and her own sense of weakness frighten her.

'What's come over you, Earl? I thought you were just a kid. So harmless —'

'I guess I've grown up. That's all.'

'I'm going to Jacob,' says Sharon with decision. 'I'm going to tell him everything.'

Earl merely smiles. He doesn't believe her. She moves toward the door and pauses, undecided.

'Go ahead,' Earl mocks her, 'tell him I'm a bad boy. Tell him you'll feed his chickens. Tell him you're through with the Star and Garter. Tell him you don't want any more nice clothes, any more jewelry, any more fun —'

Sharon bursts into tears. Earl puts his arms around her. She breaks from him and opens the door.

Outside, there is a child's scream and the sounds of crying and general dismay. Sharon runs out, followed by Earl, to see what has happened.

One of the colored children, running down the stairs, has fallen and twisted his ankle. It is not a very serious injury, but the child is in pain and crying and frightened. He has to be taken home at once and insists that 'Uncle Jacob' shall come along and not leave his side for a moment. So the scene which might have followed between Jacob and Sharon never takes place.

The party breaks up, amidst hasty good-byes, and

Jacob drives away with George and the children; leaving Sharon and Earl together, looking after him. Sharon's face is the picture of irresolution, doubt, guilt, and dismay.

PART SIX

Next morning, Sharon has an interview with the manager of the Star and Garter. The manager is rather embarrassed. He has asked Sharon to come and talk to him because he wants to make certain alterations in the program of the floor show. He has a new singer, who is to be featured. Sharon is still to appear, but only in a small way, during the opening number.

When Sharon indignantly protests, he becomes less polite. It seems that he has had several complaints and unfavorable comments from important guests. Nobody likes Sharon's singing. It just isn't good enough. The manager reminds her that he only gave her this chance because he is such a good friend of the Medwin family and because she had the backing of Earl's money. But, after all, he has to run his business and please the patrons. If she failed to make a hit, that isn't his fault. She had every opportunity. She started with everything in her favor and lots of advance publicity. He's sorry, but that's the way it is. If it weren't for Earl, he hints, he wouldn't keep her in the show at all.

Sharon, in the first shock of angry disappointment, tells him that she doesn't want any favors. If that's how he feels, she's quitting. The manager doesn't try to dissuade her. He is obviously rather relieved.

Sharon, fighting her tears, takes a taxi to the Medwins'. She finds Earl at home. Her first question is, 'Where's Jacob?'

Earl tells her that he is still somewhere downtown. He didn't come home yesterday night. Probably he'll show up later.

Sharon begins to cry. Earl is charming and sympathetic. He already knows what has happened; the manager just telephoned him, probably because he wanted to tell Earl his side of the story before Sharon told hers. Earl has had time to get ready for this scene and he has made his own plans.

When she is a little calmer, he tells her not to worry. They'll figure out something. Meanwhile, he is going to cheer her up. He has a surprise for her. How would she like to spend a day in Nevada? He has chartered a private plane at the airport. The pilot will fly them to Las Vegas, and they can come back in the evening. It will be lots of fun.

Sharon responds to his mood, at first rather unwillingly, then with increasing enthusiasm. The idea is exciting and glamorous and just fits in with the escapist instinct which always follows a bitter disappointment. Earl insists that she take a couple of drinks 'to snap her out of it,' and soon Sharon is bright-eyed and ready for adventure. Half an hour later, they start for the airport.

★   ★   ★

The afternoon and evening at Las Vegas are like a wild, highly colored dream. Earl exerts himself to the utmost to make Sharon forget her disappointment. He has never been gayer or more charming. They gamble at the roulette tables, and Earl wins and wins. It seems somehow ridiculous that a millionaire should be so lucky. They drink a good deal. And Earl insists on buying Sharon all sorts of absurd presents – Indian blankets, headdresses, huge silver bracelets, toys, souvenirs. Sharon laughs and protests that she can never take them with her; they will make the plane too heavy to fly home. So Earl gives them all away again, to strangers in the street. They become the center of a crowd, laughing, and attracted by the high spirits of the good-looking young couple.

Later that evening they sit alone at a table in a corner of a restaurant. Earl puts his arm around her, and she doesn't resist.

'Sharon, darling,' he whispers, 'why couldn't it always be like this? Just us two, having fun? I know what you're going to say – Jacob. But Jacob doesn't need you the way I do. Jacob will never need anybody. He stands on his own feet. He goes where he wants, does what he wants. I couldn't ever be like that. I get so lonesome and scared, when I'm by myself . . .'

Earl's tone becomes very soft and pleading. 'Sure, I know Jacob's wonderful. Maybe he's a kind of a saint, or something. But we're not saints, and we never will be. We're young, and we want the same things, and we laugh at the same jokes. Maybe you don't feel the same way about me you do about Jacob – I wouldn't even want you to. You like me the way a girl likes a boy. That's something, isn't it? And you like the things that money can buy – why shouldn't you? I've got money, and I want to spend it on you. What do you say, honey? Will you let me?'

Sharon doesn't answer. Earl presses closer to her. Her face becomes serious and thoughtful.

'Sharon,' he whispers coaxingly, 'I want you so much. I've got to have you. Say yes, honey. Please say yes.'

Jacob doesn't get back to the Medwins' until late that evening. He finds Mrs Medwin in a state of great excitement. Earl hasn't returned home. He has left no word of his intended plane trip to Nevada. All Mrs Medwin knows is that he is out some place with Sharon. She fears an automobile accident or some other disaster. But her chief reaction is that no one has any consideration for her feelings.

'Going off like that . . . never saying a word . . . Do people *want* me to suffer?'

As it grows later, her nervousness mounts. She phones the police and the city hospitals. Finally, she retires to her room in a state of hysteria which she imagines is caused by her anxiety, but is actually due to selfish fury. How *dare* Earl treat her like this?

Around four o'clock in the morning, the telephone rings. A long-distance call from Las Vegas for Mr Ericson.

Sharon's voice sounds queer, desperate, faraway. 'Is

that you, Jacob? Earl's had an attack . . . The doctor says it's serious . . . his heart. He wants to see you. He keeps asking . . . Jacob, I'm so scared . . . Can you come right away? There's a plane we chartered. It's flying back now. If you call the airport, they'll know about it. Everything's arranged . . . And – listen, Jacob, don't tell Mrs Medwin. Earl says not to . . . I'll explain when I see you . . . Jacob – please hurry . . .'

But Mrs Medwin has been listening to the call on her bedroom phone. Jacob has barely had time to hang up before she appears, furious and distraught. She is furious with everybody, including Jacob, whom she regards as a partner in the conspiracy against her. But for the moment she needs him. She is coming along, of course. Nobody is going to come between her and her boy. 'I *knew* this would happen!' she sobs, and her tone is almost triumphant.

The airport is called. And the two of them leave the house without further delay.

Sharon meets them at the door of Earl's hotel bedroom. She is very pale and has been crying. She avoids Jacob's eyes. They stand in silence outside the room with the doctor, while Mrs Medwin goes in to see her son.

The boy who is lying on the bed is scarcely recognizable as the charming, persuasive, romantic Earl of the previous scene. Even our first sight of him when Jacob came to the Medwins', has not prepared us for this pitiful spectacle. Earl's heart attack has altogether broken his morale. He had believed himself cured, and now the bottom has dropped out of his world again, and he is terrified.

Mrs Medwin swoops down upon him in a flutter of maternal emotion.

'Darling boy – everything's all right now – Mother's here – Mother's beside you –'

But Earl hardly seems aware of her presence.

'It's come back –' he whispers, terrified. And he stares at the window curtain which is stirring in the breeze.

We see, or half see, what Earl imagines. From his angle, the curtain seems to form itself into a shrouded, wavering figure, indescribably terrifying in its very indistinctness. Something waiting, hovering on the threshold of the visible world. Some half-embodied fear gradually assuming a hideous outer form.

'Darling – you're only imagining things. Shut your eyes. Rest. It's all right. Mother's here –' Mrs Medwin coos, with the assurance of one who sees nothing.

'I can see it,' Earl persists. 'Even when I shut my eyes. It's worse then.'

Then, gripping her arm with sudden desperation, he asks, 'Where's Jacob?'

'He's here,' Mrs Medwin admits rather unwillingly. 'You shall see him when you feel better. Mother's with you now.'

'I've got to see him now, this minute!'

'Darling, I think you'd much better wait –'

'Bring him now!' Earl tells her with such urgency that she rises and goes to the door.

'You can talk to him just for a moment,' she tells Jacob. 'But don't stay. Don't excite him.'

Jacob follows her into the room. Mrs Medwin, unwilling to surrender her maternal rights, even for a moment, hovers in the background. But Earl tells her to leave them alone.

'Jacob,' he gasps, 'it's come back. The thing at the window . . .'

Jacob kneels down beside the bed. He lays his hand on Earl's heart.

'That's because you called it back,' he says softly. 'You can send it away again.'

'I can?'

'Of course you can. You can send it away forever.'

Earl stares in front of him for a moment, with a look of intense pain and effort on his face. 'I can't –' he gasps, at length. 'It's still there.'

'Not like that,' Jacob tells him, putting his arm protectively around the terrified boy. 'Don't try to force it. Let go. You're holding it there. Let it go. Let it go.'

He passes his hand slowly over Earl's heart. Earl's tense muscles begin to relax. He sinks back, resting more easily. An expression of wonder and joy come into his face.

'Jacob – it's gone!'

'Sure. It's gone. You let it go.'

'It was so easy . . . I'd forgotten . . . The way you

105

showed me −' He manages a smile. 'It's all so simple, really.'

Jacob smiles at him. 'Your mother said not to talk. You've got to rest up.'

But something is troubling Earl. 'Jacob −?'

'Yes?'

'There's one thing I've got to tell you now − right away. I − I don't know how to begin −'

'It can wait, can't it?' Jacob asks soothingly.

'No' − Earl's agitation increases − 'it can't wait. I've got to tell you. Oh, Jacob −' Suddenly Earl's face contracts with a spasm of pain. His body twists. His hands clutch Jacob's.

'Forgive me −' he gasps out. Then he sinks back exhausted.

After a long while he opens his eyes. He seems mildly surprised to see Jacob still beside him.

'What happened?' he asks.

'Don't talk. Just relax. Try to let go.'

Earl seems to return to full consciousness for a moment. He says, very quietly and distinctively, 'I'm going to die.'

Jacob is silent, watching him with eyes full of gentleness. Earl gives him a sudden smile.

'Jacob − you cured me − after all.'

Jacob's eyes have tears in them. Slowly he shakes his head.

But Earl still smiles. His face has become calm and radiant.

'You cured me . . . Not my heart . . . that doesn't matter . . . You cured me of being afraid —'

Then another spasm, much less violent, passes over him. His head falls back.

Jacob goes quickly to the door and opens it. Mrs Medwin pushes past him into the room, followed by the doctor and Sharon.

'Earl, darling —' Mrs Medwin falls on her knees beside the bed. 'What is it? What's the matter? Earl — it's Mother. Speak to me! It's Mother, darling —' Then, as the truth dawns on her, she breaks out into loud, horrified sobbing.

The doctor bends over the bed and makes a brief examination. After a moment he looks up, indicating to Jacob and Sharon that it is all over.

In the midst of this tableau, there is a knock on the door. It is the hotel manager. He is very apologetic. He didn't wish to intrude. He only wanted to speak to Mrs Medwin. The doctor signs to him that Mrs Medwin is in no condition to speak to anybody just now. The manager, puzzled and embarrassed, whispers that he meant the other Mrs Medwin. He indicates Sharon.

Mrs Medwin looks up quickly from the deathbed. Her sobbing is cut short by an even more violent emotion.

'What do you mean?' she demands in a harsh, unnatural voice. 'What other Mrs Medwin? There isn't any other.'

Everybody looks at Sharon. After a moment's pause, she says tonelessly, 'Earl and I were married last night.'

Jacob utters an involuntary exclamation. She doesn't look at him. There is a deadly silence in the room.

Then Mrs Medwin springs to her feet. She is trembling all over – absolutely transfigured with fury.

'What a fool I was! I might have known this would happen! Why didn't I throw you out of the house the first time I set eyes on you? Yes – I see it all now! You were both in the plot together. You tried to steal my darling boy away from me – the only thing I had left in the world . . . You – you dirty, cheap little gold digger! Well – you didn't succeed. He's still mine – and he'll be mine always! You can't take him away now! Rather than see him married to you – I'm glad, I'm glad he's lying here dead!'

She throws herself down, sobbing, upon the corpse, and clasps it frantically in her arms.

There is a moment's pause. Then Jacob turns abruptly, with averted face, and strides out of the room.

As he reaches the head of the staircase, he hears Sharon's voice behind him, urgent and desperate.

'Jacob!'

He turns, then moves as if to go on.

'Jacob – where are you going?'

He doesn't answer. Sharon hurries after him, catches his arm.

'Jacob – don't go away like that! I must talk to you.'

He stops and looks at her squarely for the first time. 'What is there to say?'

'I've got to explain – I've got to make you understand, somehow –'

'I guess I understand, all right.'

'No, you don't. You don't understand a thing . . . Listen – we were both of us crazy last night. I didn't know what I was doing . . . It was like some kind of a joke – so easy – just signing our names . . . ' Sharon laughs suddenly, rather hysterically. 'Mrs Earl C. Medwin, Junior . . . Just another of Earl's jokes . . .'

She is laughing and sobbing.

'Stop that!' says Jacob sharply, catching her by the wrist. His tone is like a smack in the face. Sharon obediently controls herself.

After a moment he says, more gently, 'You loved him, didn't you?'

'I don't know . . . No. Not what *you'd* call love, Jacob . . . He was such a kid. So full of life . . . I never meant it to happen like that . . . I – well, I guess I thought I had everything under control . . . And I hadn't . . .'

Jacob says nothing.

'Jacob,' says Sharon timidly, after a pause, 'we didn't mean to hurt you, either of us.' She looks up at him. 'Will you believe that?'

'Sure,' says Jacob wearily, 'I believe it.'

He turns from her and goes slowly down the stairs.

Sharon stands looking after him hopelessly. She doesn't even try to stop him.

A year later, Jacob is visiting Earl's grave in a large,

tree-shaded cemetery on the outskirts of the city. He lays a small bunch of flowers on the tomb. Then his eye is caught by a squirrel which has come down from a neighboring tree. He pulls some peanuts out of his pocket and lures the animal toward him, talking to it in a low gentle tone as he does so. Soon it is eating out of his hand and running over his shoulders.

The sound of footsteps makes him turn his head.

Sharon is standing behind him.

His exclamation of surprise is not entirely pleasurable. Even now, we realize, it is painful for him to see her again.

'George told me I'd find you here today,' she says.

'He never told *me* anything,' says Jacob. 'He never even said he'd been seeing you.'

Sharon smiles. 'I asked him not to. I wanted to give you a surprise.'

She sits down beside him on the grass. For a few moments they talk conversationally, avoiding any dangerous subject. We learn that Jacob has been out on the desert. He had another job on a ranch. He has just returned to Los Angeles for a few days, to visit George and his family. George doesn't work at the Medwins' anymore.

Then their talk peters out. There is a long silence.

'And all this time,' Sharon asks hesitantly, 'you've been . . . alone? I mean – hasn't there been anybody – any girl?'

'There hasn't been anybody,' says Jacob briefly.

'There hasn't for me, either.'

Jacob says nothing. But we can see that he reacts to this.

'Jacob,' says Sharon softly, 'do you feel . . . that way about me still? After all that's happened?'

'Does it matter?' Jacob won't look at her.

'It matters to me,' Sharon tells him gently.

'It does?' Quickly he turns his head with an involuntary joyful smile.

'Jacob, if you could somehow forget all this – I don't mean at once – one day – and if you wanted me . . . it'd be so wonderful –'

'Sharon –!' His face shines with joy.

'You know, Jacob,' Sharon goes on, taking his hand, 'I'm a rich woman now. I could help you in all kinds of ways. That's what Earl would want, I know. We could build a clinic. You could have patients come to you from all over the country. I'd be with you all the time. Maybe I could study – share your work with you, somehow –'

But Jacob's face has fallen during this speech.

'The Medwin millions!' he says with unwonted sarcasm.

'Jacob – you wouldn't refuse? Just because it's Earl's money? That wouldn't be like you. That wouldn't be fair to him. Why – it would be like taking revenge.'

'Not because it's Earl's money,' Jacob slowly replies, choosing his words. 'Not because it's anybody's. It's just money, that's all. Money only makes money, and advertising, and success, and your name in the newspapers . . .

111

I'm no good at explaining, Sharon. I just know I can't do things that way. It would grow too big for me to handle. It would hurt people. Even if I cured a few. Even the ones I cured. It would turn into a big, fat, successful lie. I can't do it, Sharon. It's not *right*.' He pauses, then says simply, 'I don't want anybody's money, Sharon. I want you. Nothing else. You the way you were at the Carter Ranch.'

Sharon's eyes have filled with tears. 'I – guess I'm not that way anymore, Jacob.'

'Yes, you are. Underneath, you are. I can feel it.' He pauses. 'Come away with me, Sharon – when you're ready to. Leave the money behind. We don't need it.'

Sharon is deeply distressed, torn by conflicting feelings. This makes her speak quite angrily: 'Do you always have to have your own way? You're so proud – do you know that? Underneath all that gentleness, you're the proudest person I ever knew! Why can't we do it *my* way? Why can't we be comfortable, and have a nice home and nice things and not have to worry all the time where the next ten cents are coming from? Is that so wrong? Do you *want* me to slave and lose my looks and get ugly? It's just your damned obstinacy and pride.'

'Sharon,' says Jacob very patiently, 'you don't undersand . . . That's not pride. If we kept that money, we wouldn't be ourselves. You wouldn't be you. I wouldn't be me. We'd be the slaves of the money. Do you want that?'

'I'm sorry.' Sharon is penitent at once. 'I shouldn't

have spoken that way. I didn't mean it. It was just because – because I'm upset . . . You see, Jacob, there's something you don't know. I should have told you right from the start . . . But somehow I couldn't . . .' She hesitates. 'I've got a child.'

Jacob stares at her in astonishment.

'It's a boy. He's called Charles – that was Earl's middle name, you know.'

Jacob says nothing.

'I wanted to have him named Jacob,' Sharon continues. 'I think Earl would have liked that. But you see, it would have hurt' – she pauses self-consciously over the word – 'Mother.'

'Mother?' Jacob echoes, not understanding.

'Mrs Medwin,' Sharon explains with a touch of embarrassment. 'She's asked me to call her that.'

'You mean she's not mad at you anymore?'

'Not since she knew Charles was coming.' Sharon obviously realizes that Jacob is going to find this hard to understand. 'You see – Earl was all she had. You know how she felt about him. Well, now there'll be someone to take his place . . . She wants to help me raise him.'

'And you'll let her?'

'Why not? He's her grandson.'

'You'll let her –' Jacob repeats incredulously, 'after what she did to Earl?'

'Jacob – you've no right to say that!'

'It's true, isn't it?' says Jacob bluntly. 'Do you want your kid coddled and fussed over? Do you want him

113

brought up wrapped in cotton? Do you want all the strength sucked out of him before he's a man?'

'I'll see that doesn't happen . . . After all, Jacob, he'll have a marvelous education. The best of everything.'

'A lot of fancy schooling,' says Jacob scornfully. 'To teach him how to waste his money.'

'You needn't sneer at education,' exclaims Sharon hotly, 'just because you never had any.'

But Jacob is too much in earnest to be sidetracked into a quarrel. 'Sharon – we've got to raise that kid ourselves. For Earl's sake. Don't you see? We *must*. We'll take him some place away out in the desert or the mountains, where he can be with things that are alive. Not dead things. Not chairs and tables and automobiles. We'll work for him. Sure, we'll send him to school. He shall have the best schooling of any kind in the country. But no frills. No fancy stuff . . . Gosh, I'm glad about that kid, Sharon! It'll give us something to live for.'

Sharon looks at him all the time he is talking. Her face lights up for a moment. Then a look of extreme pain and sadness comes over it. Slowly she shakes her head.

'It's no good, Jacob. I can't –'

'What do you mean?'

'I can't . . . that's all. For a minute, when you said it, it sounded so wonderful. But it wouldn't work out . . . You see, it isn't only the kid. It's this life. It's having money, clothes, nice things . . . It's done something to me, Jacob. I couldn't be without it anymore.'

'You mean,' says Jacob dully, 'it's all over – with us?'

114

Sharon nods, her eyes full of tears. 'I can't go your way, Jacob. And you can't go mine. Even if I tried, it wouldn't be any use. I see that now. I'd only make us both miserable . . . I guess we'd better say good-bye.'

'Sharon' – there is a note of entreaty in Jacob's voice – 'I'm not asking for myself, but . . . do you know what you're going to do to *yourself*? Do you know what you'll be like ten years from now? Do you?'

'Maybe I do . . . I can't help it . . . Oh, Jacob, don't make it harder for me . . . And – think about me sometimes, will you?'

'Every day of my life,' says Jacob gravely.

'Good-bye, Jacob.'

'Good-bye, Sharon.'

She turns to go blindly, hardly able to see through her tears.

Then once more she faces him, sobbing. 'Think about me the way I used to be in the desert . . . I was so dumb. I didn't know . . . Jacob – I wish – I wish you'd never cured me!'

She hurries away, down the long avenue, with bowed head.

Jacob stands mournfully looking after her.

EPILOGUE

Jacob's face, the face of the middle-aged man of the Prologue, is as somber and thoughtful as when we last saw it. One may assume that all the events we have just witnessed have been passing through his mind, with the lightning speed of memory, in a few moments. When he speaks, it is in continuation of the words with which the Prologue ended.

'Take up thy bed and walk,' Jacob murmurs, speaking more to himself than to the man and woman who are watching him. 'There's plenty who can say that . . . but how many can tell when it's right to say it? How many can tell where the sick man's going, when he gets up from his sickbed? How many know what the sickness meant? It's easy enough to cure the body. But how many can cure the soul?'

Jacob is still sitting on the bench with the dog in his lap. The man and the woman watch him in silence.

'Our Lord said, 'Thy sins be forgiven thee.' He had the power. He *knew*. He saw what would happen to that man. That's why He could say it. I say, 'Arise and walk' – and I don't know anything. I'm in the dark. Maybe it's good. Maybe it's bad. I can't tell . . . People say it *must* be good. I used to think so, too. Now I can't be sure . . .'

There is a long silence. Jacob's hands have stopped moving.

Suddenly the little dog sits up in his lap and barks eagerly.

'She'll be all right now,' Jacob tells them in a matter-of-fact voice.

'Why, how wonderful!' the woman exclaims, picking up the dog. 'Why, Topsy darling, you're cured! Look, Allan, isn't it a miracle? Look at her eyes! She's perfectly well!'

'You'd best give her something to eat,' says Jacob in the same tone. And he calls to the man in the beekeeper's veil, who has just appeared around the corner of the house. 'Where did we put those dog biscuits?'

'I got them right here in my hand,' says the man in his pleasant voice. 'I kind of thought you might be needing them.'

He gives the biscuits to the woman and raises his veil. It is George, the Medwins' former chauffeur.

'I'm sure I don't know how we can ever thank you,' the woman gushes to Jacob. 'Isn't there – I mean – how much do you usually charge?'

'Nothing,' says Jacob briefly.

'Nothing? Oh, but surely –'

'I don't make a business out of this. George and I sell eggs and fruit. And we do odd jobs around for the neighbors. We get by – don't we, George?'

'Sure do,' George grins.

'Well — in that case —' the woman hesitates, then impulsively unpins some expensive flowers she is wearing on her dress. 'Won't you please take these?'

Jacob seems very pleased. He sniffs them appreciatively and arranges them carefully in an empty can. George carries them into the house.

'Well, good-bye, Mr Ericson,' says the woman, picking up her dog. 'And thank you again. It's been wonderful meeting you. If Topsy gets sick again, may we come and see you?'

'Sure. Any time,' says Jacob, shaking hands.

The man and the woman get into the car and drive away.

Now that they are alone together in the car we sense that their mood has changed. They are no longer tense and petulant, as in the earlier scene. Both are thoughtful. Their faces are relaxed and happy.

'You know,' says the husband at length, 'there's something about that guy. Something wonderful. Just being with him — it did something to me.'

'To me, too,' the woman agrees. She glances quickly at her husband. 'Allan —'

'Yes, Mary?'

'I think — maybe — it wasn't only Topsy he cured.'

Her husband smiles understandingly. 'That's just what I was thinking myself.'

'Darling — couldn't we maybe start all over? The way we used to be? It isn't too late, is it?'

The man gives her a tender smile. Then he puts his arm around her and draws her closer to him.

'No,' he says, 'it isn't too late.'

The car moves slowly down the valley.

Jacob and George stand looking after it, side by side. Both of them are smiling.